TRUSTING THE ALPHA

COURTNEY DAVIS

5 PRINCE PUBLISHING
5PRINCEBOOKS.COM

Digital ISBN: 978-1-63112-407-5

Print ISBN: 978-1-63112-408-2

Cover design by Marianne Nowicki

Interior design by 5 Prince Publishing

First Edition 042425v.1

For more information about this title, visit: www.5princebooks.com

To the man in my life who always supports my dreams.

ACKNOWLEDGMENTS

Thank you to my amazing editor, Cate, and everyone at 5 Prince Publishing who helps me to turn my stories into final products to be proud of!

Also by Courtney Davis

The Atlantis Series

The Vampires of Atlantis

Aristotle's Wolves

Descendants of Atlantis

Stand Alone Titles

Butterfly Kisses

The Serpent and the Firefly

A Spider in the Garden

Princess of Prias

Soul Sacrifice

A Shadow Among the Stars

Demons and Tea Leaves

Trusting the Alpha

Trusting the Alpha

Prologue: Susan and Paul

Susan paced the floor of her rundown trailer. She'd put the kids to bed and started drinking heavily. It had become a nightly routine. Paul was out, likely fucking a twenty-something wolf who was everything she wasn't—everything he resented her for not being.

Susan was just a human, and Paul was the alpha of this pack. Which, lately, he ran like his own personal harem, no longer caring to save her feelings or her dignity by hiding his indiscretions. Because she wasn't enough, and never would be. His wolf had chosen the wrong mate, and they were stuck with each other until one of them died.

When she heard Paul's snowmobile stop out front, Susan opened the trailer door, swaying just enough to make her reach out for the doorframe. Her head was spinning from the alcohol she'd consumed, and she had to blink to focus on the dark form surrounded by white in front of her. It was the middle of winter, and it was freezing, everything covered in so much snow she couldn't even go anywhere, which led to more time dwelling on the unfairness of this situation. Paul didn't care that she was depressed, they were far north in Canada with lots of room for the wolves to roam, and nowhere for a human among them to find companionship, or help. She was sure he'd chosen this place partially so she'd be alone and completely reliant on him.

Paul adjusted his crotch and sneered at her as he walked toward the house. She truly hated him in that moment, and when he stepped into the circle of light surrounding the porch and she saw a new hickey on the front of his neck, she accepted that he truly hated her too. This marriage was a sham and although it hadn't always been, she accepted that it always would be. She wanted out.

His eyes were dark, his wolf subdued, and it was just his human self that faced her now with a sneer. She threw her half full drink at him, but he only laughed and swatted it away, the glass shattering on the nearby ice.

"You're an asshole!" she screamed at the man she had at one time been deeply in love with.

Their marriage hadn't started out bad of course, they'd met and dated, and she'd fallen in love. They married and she gave him two strong wolf shifter children. She was told she couldn't have any more after that due to trouble birthing their daughter, and ever since then Paul treated her like an unwanted extra in their lives. That's when he stopped hiding what he really was—a lecherous beast.

She couldn't even leave him because he said he'd kill her if she tried to keep the kids and she was afraid of leaving them here with him as their only parent. She was afraid their son would grow up to be just like his father. She was afraid their daughter would suffer just like she was with a wolf shifter mate who was violent and uncaring.

"Go back inside woman. You're drunk," he commanded.

A part of her wanted to listen, she could feel through the mating bond that he expected her to listen. She didn't have to be a wolf to feel the effects of his supernatural control, one of the many things he'd neglected to tell her before saying *I do.* But what he probably hadn't expected was that her not being a wolf meant she could resist it.

Most of the time she listened anyway, because the alternative usually resulted in humiliation. He would spend days away in the bed of another and she'd have to explain to her kids why their father was missing. She'd have to endure the knowing looks and whispers of the pack. But not tonight. She was tired of his shit, tired of the looks of pity she got from the pack and she was drunk enough to tell him so.

"What the fuck is wrong with you, Paul? You have a family here, a wife and kids, what the hell are you doing?"

He growled at her, his eyes slightly yellow and threatening, his wolf was trying to push to the surface through the fog of whatever drugs he had taken. Usually the two parts of a wolf shifter worked together, the wolf and human, though they were capable of separate thoughts and desires, or so Paul had explained to her when he'd revealed himself to her on their wedding night. But usually one or the other was in the most control, and the tell was in the eyes more than the physical form. Yellow eyes meant his wolf was taking over, dark eyes meant his wolf was sitting back, observing from within.

She wasn't as afraid of his wolf as she was of his human self. His wolf still had the mate instinct, still wished to protect her and right now the wolf wanted her to listen to him. He wanted her inside where she would be warm and safe. A part of her wanted to accept what the animal was insisting, but she couldn't forget the human part of him too, and she knew her husband resented her for calling him out on his actions. She knew he wasn't about to stop sleeping around no matter how it angered and embarrassed her.

Susan knew Paul wasn't likely to hurt her physically, the wolf wouldn't allow that. But he'd hurt her for years, over and over again every time he fucked someone else, and she had to sit at pack events getting sympathetic looks from the other females, knowing they'd slept with her husband. Why hadn't the wolf stopped him? Susan didn't really understand how these shifters worked, she was a human and could never be what they are, but her children were, and some days she hated that fact. She didn't want them to be like him.

"You're worthless as a husband and father, why don't you go cool off in the lake," she snapped.

"What did you say to me, you ungrateful bitch?" He took a threatening step forward and for the first time in almost twenty years, she worried for her life in his presence. There wasn't enough yellow in his eyes, the wolf was still being suppressed.

"Did you take something tonight?" she demanded.

"I take whatever the hell I want," he snarled and lurched toward her. "You don't tell me what to do, I'm *alpha*." His eyes flickered between brown and yellow as he struggled with his wolf for control.

Susan stumbled back, afraid that this time, his wolf wouldn't be strong enough to stop Paul. There was an intense glassiness to his eyes as he got closer that she'd never seen before, he'd definitely taken something strong. She had to stop him, she had to reach his wolf and get him to back off. She thought of the kids inside asleep and fear of what they could wake up and witness pushed her to lash out without thinking.

"Go jump in the lake, Paul," she ordered, her voice as firm and strong as she could manage, making sure his wolf knew she was serious. She wanted him away from her, away from the kids. She wanted him to wash off the smell of the other woman and sober up.

And part of her wanted him to die, to leave them alone for good and a part of her was terrified of being left alone with the pack and children. She couldn't make herself take it back though. She tilted up her chin and stared at him, waiting for him to beg and apologize and make empty promises about changing his ways. She quickly realized he would never do that, he hadn't in the past and he would not now, he didn't think he was doing anything wrong and she loathed him more in that moment than she had in their entire failed marriage.

. . .

Paul struggled for a moment, frozen between his wolf's desire to obey his mate's command and his human desire to harm her for existing, for not being what he thought he deserved. She wasn't strong enough, she couldn't even give him more children, and he felt like he deserved so much more than what she was. He was an *alpha*, he should have mated to the best wolf shifter there was, not a human whose body gave out after only two pups.

His wolf fought against those human thoughts, it had always tried to convince Paul that Susan was perfect if only Paul could let go of his ideals about what an alpha should be, could be, needed to be. But all Paul knew was what his father and grandfather had shown him. They had ruled with an iron control and with the most desired female wolf ruling beside them.

He was glad his father and grandfather had both passed away before he'd found Susan, he couldn't imagine the humiliation that he would have felt to introduce a human as his mate.

Tonight, in the face of his mate's demand, his human anger lost the battle despite the drugs he'd taken. Paul shifted to wolf and took off toward the frozen lake. His wolf was desperate to get away from her so he wouldn't harm her. And because of the fucking mate bond, his wolf was helpless against her order, he had to obey and it gave his wolf the strength it needed to fight past the haze of drugs to gain control.

Paul saw the frozen lake and increased his speed. Susan's order ran through his head again and the hurt and anger in her eyes fueled him further. At one time he'd loved her enough, thought that she'd be enough, thought his wolf had to be right about their mate. At one time he'd entered into the bond of mate with her eagerly, but it had gone to shit almost immediately. He'd realized after he revealed his true self to her that she couldn't handle all that he was, and then it was too late. They were married, he'd bitten her and cemented the link between her and his wolf and then they were forever connected until death.

Death.

A part of him relished the idea of leaving everything behind that was hard, that was wrong, and that he kept fucking up. There had been many times over the years when his human side had wished for death, wished to just end it all, all the suffering he went through, all the suffering he couldn't save his pack from. The only thing that had kept a gun out of his mouth had been his wolf, it insisted that they survive to protect his mate and pack. Now it was his wolf who strode toward that end with an eagerness that surprised them both. His wolf was happy to obey its mate this one last time.

He thought of his children and almost faltered in his step. Ruben would take care of them, and the pack, until Mick was old enough to take over as alpha. Ruben was a good wolf, a good man. He was Paul's youngest brother and he hadn't witnessed the same violence Paul had, hadn't experienced the cruel way their father and grandfather had ruled the pack. How they had destroyed enemy packs that dared to come too close. Ruben was the last-born child before a sickness swept through all the North America packs and brought the species near extinction. It had left Paul as the oldest son and so, the alpha. A position that never should have been his but he'd embraced.

Would any of his deceased brothers have done a better job? Would they have mated to a wolf shifter instead of a weak human and found a way to fix their broken pack?

Paul's last thought before jumping as far out into the icy water as he could go was of his young son. He prayed to whatever god might be willing to listen to the last wish of a fuck-up like him, that Mick found the kind of perfect partnership that would make his life easy. A perfect wolf to mate with an alpha and rule the pack.

When he landed and sunk into the cold water it was a shock to his system and he started to struggle, human instincts of survival finally kicking in. The alcohol and drugs in his system made him slow and he gulped in a mouthful of sharp icy water knowing this was it. His wolf was silent in his mind, this was its last act of protection for its mate.

Susan had killed him, and he hoped she died from the guilt.

Susan stared into the night after her husband and the sounds of wolves howling surrounded her. It was such a mournful noise; it could mean only one thing. Their alpha was dead.

She stumbled inside and grabbed the gun from Paul's bedside table then looked out the window. Yellow eyes stared back at her with rage and the howls of sorrow became snarls promising retribution. She looked back to where her children slept on, and tears rolled down her face. "Take care of Mick and Tara," she whispered.

A shot rang out in the night and two children were left alone.

CHAPTER 1

MICK

Mick sat up in bed, gasping and sweating; the remembered sound of a gunshot reverberated in his skull. It was a familiar nightmare and one that most recently was haunting him because of his decision to wed.

The sunlight streaming into his bedroom held the tint of early dawn, but already he could hear his pack going about their lives. They were happy sounds that reinforced why he'd chosen to move the pack here when he'd taken over as alpha, and why he was fighting so hard for them to be able to stay here.

Mick walked out into the cool morning; summer in Idaho. He sat on the front porch of his cabin and waved at a group of pack kids kicking a ball back and forth. This place used to be a boy scout camp. Tucked away in the mountains and near a lake; it had a large clubhouse they'd turned into a bar and grill, and five small cabins around a large clearing with a bonfire setup complete with seating and picnic tables.

After moving the pack here, they'd built some larger cabins further back for families. He supposed he'd need to build one for himself sooner rather than later. He loved kids, always wanted some, even if he was afraid that he'd be as crappy a father as his own had been. He thought of his late uncle, Ruben, who had stepped in to raise him and Tara when their parents both died. It reminded Mick that there was another way for a father figure to be. When Ruben had taken on the care of Mick and Tara he'd given them love and safety like they'd never experienced before.

That was what Mick would model his own family after when he had the chance.

His sister, Tara emerged from her little cabin and walked over with two cups of coffee in hand, giving him one with a grunt. "Couldn't sleep?" she asked.

"No, keep dreaming about Mom and Dad," he admitted.

She nodded, understanding everything and she didn't press for details or tell him it was all okay. She had her own nightmares that plagued her, more recent ones, too.

"So when is Janet coming?" Tara asked with undisguised disdain.

"I need to meet with Royal and hash out last details about the protection he's offering. Unless ..." he looked at his sister with an arched brow.

She growled. "I am not marrying that bear shifter just to keep his clan away from our pack."

"Just checking, because if I have to marry Janet and then you change your mind about Kody, I'm going to be more than a little pissed, sister."

"I'm not sure I'll ever be ready to settle down," she admitted, "especially not with someone like Kody."

Mick couldn't blame her; she'd been through some kind of hell with her ex, and he'd just been a human. He couldn't imagine what kind of trust she'd have to have in someone as physically strong as the bear shifters.

Mick sighed. "Which is why I'm doing this. As alpha, I need to put this pack first, always." It was an added bonus that the marriage to Janet would keep him from ever entering into a mate bond. He had no interest in a repeat of what his parents had put each other through. He'd been young the night they died, but he had seen enough, and heard even more as he got older. A wolf was supposed to pick the most perfect person to be their partner and spouse, the perfect other half to make strong and healthy wolf shifter children. Somehow his father's wolf had only gotten the strong wolf shifter children part right, they hadn't seemed to be suited in any other way. Maybe it had been an after effect of the sickness and near extinction of the species, but for whatever reason, it had been a toxic marriage for both of them. And there had been no way out thanks to the mating bond. His father's wolf never would have left her, and he also never would have let her leave.

It was a risk he wasn't willing to take. He wanted something more transactional, more business-like. His wolf growled disagreement through his mind and thought longingly of what so many of their packmates had.

Mick's second in command, Lance, walked up hand in hand with his mated wife, Madeline, a trail of kids following. They'd been mated and married for almost ten years and had a few kids to show for it with another one on the way. They were the epitome of mated wolf shifter bliss, happy in their bond and ridiculously in love.

Mick's wolf wanted that too, but Mick saw it as a loss of control he desperately wanted to avoid. He was willing to marry, to have kids and a wife he was responsible for, but he didn't want his wife to be able to tell his wolf what to do. He didn't want his wife and his wolf to have more say over him than his human half did. A wolf shifter who wasn't mated had two halves, the wolf and the man. They worked together, a symbiotic relationship where neither half exerted more control over the other. But if you were mated, then the wolf would do literally anything its mate told it to do whether the man agreed or not and this was true whether the man or the wolf was currently in physical form. It was a special power put in place by whatever gods had created them to assure that male wolves wouldn't harm their children, wouldn't harm their perfect mate so they could continue the species. It made it so that the animal instinct of the wolf would never become a monster and destroy everything.

At least that was the theory, he thought maybe his parents were evidence that it wasn't true.

"Good morning," Madeline called out and Lance gave him a nod.

Mick had dated Madeline fairly seriously when they were in their teens and early twenties. He had even considered marrying her eventually, knowing full well it would be a marriage without the mate bond, his wolf assured him she wasn't the one for him even though his wolf agreed she was attractive. She had long blonde curls and milky white skin. She'd been tall and slender and everything all the young wolves panted after. But her bond instinct had clicked for Lance one day out of nowhere, and that was it. Mick had let her go without hard feelings because the mating bond was involuntary and she'd been so damn happy to have found her true mate.

Now he looked at her and felt no draw to her at all, he only saw her as an important part of his pack, a friend, and someone to protect.

"How are you feeling today, Madeline?"

"Big and cranky," she grumbled. "I'm looking forward to meeting this little one in about a month."

Mick raised an eyebrow at Lance. "And you're ready for another pup, Lance?"

"As if I have a choice," Lance teased, and Madeline smacked his arm.

"You know how they're made, big boy," she growled.

He grinned wide at her. "That I do."

"Gross, get a room," Tara snarled.

"Somebody needs a date," Mick said while Lance and Madeline laughed and walked away.

"Last time I went on a date, Kody showed up and almost ate him," Tara snarled.

"Well maybe you shouldn't have had him take you to dinner in Vernon, you were shoving your date in Kody's face, what did you expect?"

Tara stared into her coffee mug and shrugged. "I guess I thought he'd get the hint that I am definitely not interested and finally stop staring over the territory line like a lovesick fool."

"You know that isn't how shifters work."

"He practically pissed on my leg in the restaurant, Mick. I won't make that mistake again."

Mick hid his laugh behind a sip of coffee. "You'll find someone, Tara. Someone who deserves you and treats you right. And when he pisses on your leg, you'll like it," he teased.

Tara growled and hit his shoulder, making his coffee slosh out onto the ground.

They stared out at the pack for a few minutes, each contemplating the future.

"But you won't," she whispered. "Not if you go through with this thing with Janet."

The pain in his sister's voice was comforting but it only drove him forward in his decision. He needed to protect her and everyone else here so they could live the life they wanted. If they let the bear shifters chase them from their territory, he wasn't sure they'd find somewhere else as perfect. They'd made this their home in a few short years. Now they had to defend it.

Mick had been in charge since Uncle Ruben died when Mick was seventeen, and he'd been determined to find a place for them to settle. It had taken twenty years, but he had, and now it was time for the other part of his duty as alpha. He needed to start making pups.

The American Wolf Shifter was still an endangered species, but it was on an upswing. The sickness that swept through before he was even born had wiped out many packs completely and most others were still struggling to recover. It meant that no one was exempt from the obligation to reproduce, especially the alpha.

Mick had always wondered if the drop in their numbers was the cause of his father's wolf mating to a human. Did the uncertain future of the species force his father's wolf to seek out something different to help ensure their future? Would diversity in their genetics have saved more wolves from the sickness? If that were true, then why hadn't more of the pack mated to humans? His father was the only one in their pack who had, and from what he knew of the few other scattered packs out there, it was just as rare for them, though it did happen.

A few hours later, Mick was sitting at a table in the clubhouse, drinking a beer and looking across at Royal.

Royal was an older wolf shifter alpha with a touch of grey in his black hair and a hard set to his mouth. He'd been running the pack that was settled north of Mick's territory for over thirty years, but he hadn't let himself get soft and his muscles bulged under a plaid shirt. Mick's wolf recognized the threat and hovered just under the surface, ready to lash out if Royal attacked. Royal's eyes were clear blue, no hint of his own wolf surfacing which made Mick feel like he was overreacting and showing his youth as weakness to the older alpha.

"Janet needs a husband, and you need protection from the bear shifters, I think it's a deal we can strike," Royal said.

"Good, I want to grow the pack here." The location was perfect. It was just unfortunate that the land was sandwiched between a bear shifter clan and a neighboring pack of wolf shifters.

"You have lost your mate?" Royal asked, eyes narrowing on Mick.

"No, never found her," Mick said.

Royal's lips thinned, not liking the answer. A wolf only got one mate so there was a real risk marrying a wolf shifter that wasn't your mate unless you both had a mate who died. It didn't mean the wolf wouldn't accept, love, and care for the spouse; it just meant that the bond that would connect them on a deeper level would never be present, and the wolf would never be fully satisfied. It was a hard sell to a wolf who was convinced its mate was out there somewhere just waiting to be discovered.

"Janet did, they were both young when the bond clicked but he was shot by a hunter on a full moon run."

"I'm sorry to hear that, I'm sure it was hard on her," he said because he knew it was the right thing to say, not that he really cared.

Royal grunted. "Why aren't you willing to wait for yours? The numbers of wolves are improving, you just might have to travel farther to find her, you likely have one out there."

"I have no interest in a mate bond," he said honestly.

Royal grunted. "You say that now, but when you meet your mate, you'll think again."

Mick just shook his head. "I am willing to commit fully to Janet, you don't have to worry about anything getting in the way of that. No mate bond is going to change my duty which is to the protection of this pack above all else. If I marry Janet, she is part of this pack."

Royal didn't look convinced, and Mick drank his beer to cover his uncertainty.

"Daddy," Janet whined, "I want to marry him." She pushed her lip out in a pout.

Mick had to force himself to look at the female. She was not what he'd have picked for himself, ever. She was short and skinny with large breasts and hip bones that jutted out too far. She was clothed so skimpily he could see everything, and it didn't make him want to take her to bed. Though he had. He hadn't been willing to propose to someone he hadn't tossed around at least once to make sure he'd be able to do his duty as a husband and alpha. The last thing he wanted was a sexless, childless marriage.

He studied her closer, wondering what their children would look like. Janet's hair was long and red, her eyes light blue much like her father's, and her skin was bronzed from the sun. She was wearing far too much makeup which made her look like the type of girl that threw herself at every male she encountered. She was likely trying to forget that the mate bond was impossible for her now. If she was willing to accept this arrangement as consolation, then he'd do what he could to make it pleasant for them both.

Royal glared at her, and she cowered, her pouting lip sucked in. Mick didn't like her instinct to cower at such a small showing from her alpha, he wanted a strong wife to give him children with strong wolves capable of leading. It was one of the reasons he'd chosen an alpha's daughter.

She flicked her gaze his way and it glowed yellow just under the surface, easing his worry. Her wolf was there, she was just used to holding it back from her father which meant he likely had some anger issues. It showed an intelligence that he could appreciate and proved she wasn't quick to anger. Two traits he'd like to see in his children.

Royal nodded at Mick. "We will be back in a couple days to set the details and then you'll have our full support against the bear clan."

Mick reached out and shook Royal's hand. He didn't spare another glance for Janet who preened and pushed her breasts forward trying to entice him, he just turned and walked back to his office, giving the other alpha his back in a show of dominance. He may need this marriage for his pack's safety, but he wasn't going to bow down to Royal as his dominant.

As soon as Mick sat behind the desk, his office door opened and Lance stepped in.

"What the hell are you thinking, you can't marry that—"

"Careful, Lance, she's going to be your alpha's wife."

Lance growled, his brown eyes flashing yellow. Mick's wolf

responded, showing itself in his eyes and Lance's retreated and he bowed his head.

"You deserve better," Lance pleaded. "Madeline loves you, and she is worried this is going to take you down a very destructive path. That you'll never truly be happy."

Mick laughed. "If Madeline loved me, this wouldn't be an issue, would it?" Bitterness entered his tone and he regretted it. "Not that I would change anything for you two, you know that."

Lance sighed. "I know. Can't stop the mate bond," Lance said with a rueful smile. "Just think about it, Mick. Make sure you're making the decision best for *you*, not just the pack. None of us would destroy your happiness for our own, you know that."

"I know," Mick said but that didn't matter, it was his duty to sacrifice his happiness for them.

Lance left and Mick leaned back in his chair, staring up at the ceiling. Lance's words filled his mind. *A very destructive path.* This was supposed to keep him off a destructive path. But he had to admit, maybe he was more like his father than he wanted to be because the thought of Janet being his wife led to thoughts of how he could reasonably sneak out to find a more appealing romp every now and then. Not in his pack—never among his people who might feel obligated to sleep with him because of his position—but perhaps in town among the humans.

CALLIE

Callie shook as she got in the car. She was trying to look casual in case any neighbors were watching but it wasn't easy, she hurt. Oliver had hit her hard last night and every facial expression, every time she tried to talk calmly to her son, she nearly cringed with pain. Her lip was split, her eye was black, and her cheek was green with an older bruise. She looked terrible and she felt even worse. Usually she'd spend the next week inside, hiding her shame and doing everything she could to keep Oliver happy while pretending to Taylor that this was all okay, that it was all normal.

She couldn't this time.

"Mom, I forgot my pencil case," Taylor cried from the back seat as she started the car.

Callie was trembling, she was prepared to leave. Oliver had been gone from the house for thirty minutes and he wouldn't return home for hours from work, but she needed every second of that time to put distance between them. She didn't want to go back into that house, ever.

"Mom," Taylor whined again.

Callie took a deep breath, "Okay, baby, I'll get it." She hurried back into the house because she needed Taylor to be okay with what they were doing, and if his pencil case would make this escape easier on him, she'd get it.

She ran past the wedding photo of her and Oliver, young and in love. She didn't resist the urge to push it off the wall, the satisfying sound of its crash spurred her on. She hurried to Taylor's room and grabbed his pencil case then rushed back through the house. Her heart was beating wildly, her breath coming in pants and her jaw ached from how hard she was gritting her teeth.

What if he comes home early? What if a neighbor sees us and calls him? What if this is my only chance and I screw it up?

Taylor's bright smile at seeing her returning with the pencil case broke her heart. This sweet young boy was more worried about leaving behind a few pencils than leaving behind his father. How had she missed the fact that there was no real bond between father and son? She supposed she should be grateful, because it meant that Taylor wouldn't want to be like his father someday. She worried she would never be able to show him what a healthy relationship should look like between a man and woman.

It hurt her to know that he'd already seen so much of the worst a man can do. That it had taken her so long to gain the strength to leave and save them both. And even now that they were leaving they were doing it without a plan and with barely any money.

But she knew it was now or never, he was going to kill her if she stayed.

CHAPTER 2

TARA

Tara followed Royal and Janet out of the clubhouse, she didn't trust either of them and she wasn't the only one. Brad and David, two other pack members, were right behind her. They all leaned casually on the front porch and watched the two outsiders get into a beat-up truck and drive away.

"Is Mick really going to go through with this?" Brad snarled.

"I wish he wouldn't," Tara agreed.

"If only there was another way to deal with the bear clan," David snapped at her and stalked off into the woods.

Tara bit her lip and looked away from Brad who huffed agreement and walked back inside.

This was partially on her, she knew it, but just the thought of doing what the others thought should be an easy sacrifice filled her with panic. If she aligned herself with the bear clan, if she gave in to what Kody wanted, she'd be putting herself at the mercy of one of the only creatures stronger than a wolf shifter.

She walked to the woods and began to strip; running in wolf form usually eased her when she started to feel this anxious. She pulled off her shirt and ran a finger along the jagged, purple scar on her abdomen.

She'd almost died because she'd trusted the wrong person. A human ... just a weak, stupid human had almost ended her. And her packmates thought she should give herself to a bear shifter who could rip her apart with his bare hands? She'd never feel safe again. It didn't matter that Kody claimed she was his mate. A fact that had started an argument one night between Tara and Allen at the diner where they both worked. Allen had taken a dirty chef's knife to her right in the hallway, no hesitation or thought for the consequences. He'd meant to kill her because he was worried someone else wanted her.

She was full of anger at how helpless she'd been that day, how she'd let her emotions override her instincts for so long and made herself vulnerable to someone so undeserving. She threw her clothes into a pile and shifted into a small black wolf then took off at a fast pace, following the perimeter of their territory. She started on the north side, along the main highway that separated their land from Royal's. She went all the way to the western edge of their territory which bordered the town of Millsburg. She smelled a lot here, so many humans, it made her sneeze. She loved that the pack lived secluded in their little spot of safety. When Mick had found the scout camp for sale it had been a godsend to the pack, they'd been living most recently in a crowded trailer park in Nevada, close to some open land, but no woods to hide and hunt in. It had been dangerous, which had kept everyone on edge and cranky.

It was just another reason Mick was trying so hard to make this place work for the pack. She, maybe more than anyone, understood his desire for safety, security, and a home. This place was ideal for the life the pack wanted to live, but the sacrifice he was willing to make was too much. She knew it was too much, but she couldn't do what was necessary to stop it. Maybe she was a coward. Maybe Mick was a great alpha because he would sacrifice anything for his pack.

Tara turned, heading east along the southern boundary. This is where they bordered the bear clan's territory.

She was halfway across when she smelled cedar and a musk she recognized that stoked her wolf's desire. She skidded to a halt when she saw the large man leaning against a tree.

"Tara," Kody growled, "I would know my mate in any form."

He was tall, close to seven feet and so wide she wasn't sure her hands would meet if she hugged him. He had long blond hair and caramel brown eyes. She didn't respond but found herself drawing in more of his scent, her wolf delighting in it.

"Won't you shift and talk to me?" Kody asked softly.

She shook her wolf head. She would not stand naked in front of this man. He wasn't pack and that meant he wasn't safe, she backed away, preparing to dart north and abandon her perimeter check.

"Wait," he pleaded. "Tara, I just want to talk. My brother, he's getting nervous about the possible union of Mick and Janet. He is trying to get more of the clan convinced that we need to remove your pack."

She growled.

"I won't let any of them hurt you, but it would be easier to convince them without violence if you'd let me claim you the way my bear wants to."

She bared her teeth at him, then ran off. She knew it was a cowardly move, she should have shifted and spoken to him, but what would it matter if she told him again, what she'd told him in the past? She had no interest in mating with him, or anyone else. She wasn't sure she would ever be able to trust someone enough to be intimate again.

Kody's pained growl followed her.

David loped into step beside her and growled, nipping at her as if to say he'd heard all that and she was wrong for not doing what was necessary to protect the pack. She ran faster, veering off to the east. She was smaller than David, but she was faster because she was able to duck through some spots where his big wolf had to go around. She made it to her clothes before him and was already pulling her pants on when he arrived and shifted. No one in the pack cared if they were naked in front of each other, it was a part of being a shifter and so he didn't even so much as glance at her breasts as he glared at her, and she felt no trepidation over her exposure or his.

The pack was the only place she felt safe anymore.

"You are being a bitch," David snapped. "You could save Mick from the worst mistake of his life but you're too selfish. I know that you're scared, and I know that you're letting your brother take the hit because you think you're too weak to control a bear mate. A *mate,* Tara. It's not like he's asking to fuck you in exchange for a deal."

She glared at him, pulled her shirt on, and stalked off toward her cabin without a word. She knew exactly what Kody wanted, and she just couldn't do it.

Her throat wanted to close up, and she just kept remembering the anger in Allen's face as he'd sliced into her, all while declaring how much he loved her. Telling her that no one but him was going to have her, that she belonged to him in life and death.

Then there was the ferocity in Kody's roar as he had torn Allen apart with his human hands as he spouted his own strikingly similar declarations; that he loved her, that she was his and he'd do anything for her.

How could she ever trust such a violent being?

KODY

Kody glared at his brother across the living room.

"Royal has agreed to the marriage," Kyr growled, holding up his phone and showing a text from Janet.

Kody held back a snarl, reminding himself that his brother was alpha and he couldn't challenge Kyr head-on unless he was ready to fight for the position, something that he'd recently felt more inclined to do.

"I'm trying to stop it; I have an alternative if only Tara would—"

"You're disgusting, Kody," Kyr interrupted with a roar. "Panting after a fucking wolf, blind to the fact that the packs uniting is going to be the end of our reign here. Royal already has a large pack, adding Mick's to it will be more than we can push against. This isn't about your dick, brother, this is about our life here, our power in this part of the country. If you want to fuck a wolf, call Janet, she's always interested."

"Why are you obsessed with this as a problem?" Kody challenged. "Royal has never tried to take our territory from us, this isn't going to change that. And if you care so much, why aren't you marrying Janet? You've slept with her plenty," Kody pointed out.

Kyr growled. "I would never debase myself like that. Taking a wolf to bed is one thing, marrying one is another. We are bear shifters, Kody, we stick to our own kind for family."

Kody disagreed—more than disagreed—he had proof that Kyr's idea was against nature because he had felt the mating call for Tara the first time he'd scented her in the woods to the north. He hadn't even laid eyes on her before he knew she was destined to be his and when he'd seen her the first time it had been overwhelming. Too bad she'd sprayed him with bear spray and took off back north and then he'd been chased out of the new wolf shifter's territory by her packmates.

"We are going to have to move against them, we can't allow this union to take place," Kyr insisted. "I wanted you to know, so if you are desperate to do something about that little dog before then, you're running out of time. Fuck her and get it over with, get her out of your system before we chase them away, or kill them."

Kody barely held himself back from attacking his brother. The way Kyr talked about Tara had him seeing red, but he didn't want to fight his brother, he wanted peace in their clan. Kody had vowed to their father on his death bed that he would support Kyr, that he would balance him out. Kyr was making it harder than ever to keep that promise.

Kyr walked out of the house with a final growl and Kody pulled out his phone. He sent off a text to Tara knowing she wouldn't respond. She never responded.

> Kyr is getting restless, doesn't like the idea of the packs uniting.

> There's one good way to fix this problem …

The little read sign came up almost instantly and his heart started to beat out of control knowing her eyes were on his words. But no little dots came, no signal that she was going to respond.

Kody threw the phone at the couch and went outside. One good way to relieve this stress was a prowl. He started to strip on the porch.

"You going hunting?" Patrice, a bear shifter that he and Kyr had grown up with asked as she walked up.

Kody scowled at the woman, he knew what this was, Kyr had sent her to distract him. Not that Patrice wasn't attractive, and he had slept with her in the past, but that had ended years before he'd scented Tara. Now it was ridiculous to even think about being with anyone else.

"Don't want company," Kody said as Patrice started to strip as well.

"You look tense, let me help," Patrice tried again, her voice low and sultry.

"Stop being a whore, Patrice, Kody isn't interested, you're sniffing the wrong asshole," Laura said, walking up to them.

Kody smiled at his best friend as she sauntered up to the porch. Laura had joined the clan about ten years ago. She had wandered into their territory with a story about her whole clan being wiped out by hunters. She was a smaller bear than the rest of them, but she was tough and her inner dominance was obvious. She didn't take anyone's shit and she didn't use her body to get a better place in the clan, Kody respected that. Kyr thought she was a major bitch and avoided her after being rejected a couple times, something else that made Kody like her.

Patrice snarled at Laura but put her shirt back on.

"Call me when you need a good time or stress relief," Patrice threw over her shoulder at Kody and winked as she swung her ass heading away.

"Gross, I can't believe you ever slept with that," Laura said.

"Yeah, me neither."

"You really don't want company? I won't suck your dick, but I'll run around and eat rabbits with you."

"No, but thanks." Kody sat down now in just his boxers and sighed heavily. "Apparently, the wolf packs are going to unite; it's got Kyr on edge and threatening violence again."

"Can't blame him for being worried, what are you going to do?"

"I want to go up there and sweep Tara up, take her somewhere private and never let her go."

"Sounds romantic, in a stalker kidnapper sort of way," Laura said with a grin.

Kody rolled his eyes. "I know, it's just instinct. If she wasn't so resistant to giving me a chance, I think I could calm some of that down enough to prove to her that I want to worship her, not destroy her."

"I don't think she's afraid of those instincts, she's a wolf, theirs are a lot the same. She's afraid of your physical ability to harm her. If she mated a wolf, they would be more evenly matched. Of course, she *was* harmed by a human so maybe she'd be just as afraid of a wolf, I don't know."

"I can't help what I am."

"And she can't help what trauma she's been through," Laura pointed out and her eyes stared off into the distance. "It doesn't always leave room for reason."

Kody reached out and touched her arm, drawing her back to the present. "Hey, you're safe here. No one hunts in our territory."

She gave him a weak smile. "Yeah, I know."

Laura walked away and Kody sighed. He wished he could save her too, but she needed to do her own healing. She was better than she'd been when she came to them, but she would probably never slough off all the trauma she was hiding, no one did.

It wasn't lost on him that Tara needed the same thing, time

and space to heal. The problem was that his bear didn't understand, and his brother was threatening both those things.

If only he could quickly prove to Tara that she could trust him.

CHAPTER 3

CALLIE

Four long and exhausting days later Callie gripped the steering wheel so tight her knuckles were white, and she'd developed callouses from the constant pressure. She was still afraid Oliver was following them so she didn't stop for more than the briefest break and with each mile she put behind them she expected to feel an easing of her worry but she didn't.

She eyed every car with suspicion and had spent the last thirty minutes trying to decide if the car following behind her with the Maine license plates could possibly be Oliver.

Had he found them?

Would he run her off the road and finally murder her like he'd threatened for the last ten years?

Would he take their son to raise the way he saw fit?

When the suspicious car had finally passed and she saw the four teenage girls in it, she had only been able to relax a little. Her body was wired for fear after years of abuse at the hands of her husband. She'd been in a constant state of anxiety for so long she wasn't sure she'd ever feel truly safe or relaxed again.

She looked in the rearview mirror and saw Taylor asleep in the back seat. He was the only thing keeping her sane through this ordeal and he was the reason she would keep searching for safety no matter how elusive it seemed. She would drive until she hit the Pacific Ocean if that's what it took.

With a steadying breath that did very little to calm her nerves, she focused on the road ahead. The sun was setting and she didn't look forward to the coming night and the decisions she'd have to make about sleep or driving through exhaustion.

Taylor groaned and sat up. Rubbing his eyes, he looked out the window and frowned. "Mountains."

"Yep, we just crossed over into Idaho."

"Sounds boring," he said.

Callie smiled at his words. According to a seven-year-old, everything except video games was boring.

"I need to go to the bathroom," he said suddenly.

Panic filled her at the thought of stopping, she hated stopping. She'd driven hours upon hours, even when she was barely able to keep her eyes open to prevent stops. They did gas, bathroom, and food all at once when necessary and she'd slept in brief stints tucked into parking lots of superstores a couple times throughout the nights. She didn't have money to waste on a hotel she'd never feel safe enough to relax in anyway. Somehow, she thought if Oliver were to bang on her car window in a brightly lit parking lot she would just be able to start the car and drive away. It felt safer than him finding her in a hotel room with no witnesses and no escape.

"Pee or not ..." she asked and watched Taylor roll his eyes in the mirror at her refusal to talk about what other things went on in the bathroom. But if he just had to pee, she'd pull to the side and let him do his business quickly there.

"Not," he said sternly. "Can we stop? I'm starving too, and I want a soda," he whined.

Tears pricked her eyes and she looked at her old leather purse in the passenger seat. She was low on funds, really low. With absolutely no plan as to what to do about it either.

Survival was still her only plan.

"Sure," she said. "I just don't know when we'll see anything." They had been driving through nothing but forested highway for the last hour and no signs indicated bathroom facilities. Taylor might have to learn the roadside squat, which in her opinion was safer than stopping anywhere with people anyway, but he'd been staunchly opposed to giving it a try in the past few days.

She knew it was completely unreasonable for her to think someone would recognize them out here in the middle of nowhere, but she couldn't help the fear. Someone who knew her or Oliver could report back to him that his wife and son were seen and then he'd be on their trail.

She'd done what she could to send him searching in another direction before they left. The last search on their home computer was for driving directions to Florida. He should be headed south to find them, unless he caught wind of them here.

Ten minutes later Taylor was bouncing in his seat and when she suggested anything other than indoor plumbing he refused.

A light ahead gave her a bit of hope and she slowed the car, put on her blinker and prayed to whatever god or goddess might be listening that no one here happened to know an asshole named Oliver Munson from Maine.

"Oh," she said as she pulled up in front of the place. There were a few motorcycles and vehicles outside and neon signs for beer in the windows. It was a log cabin style establishment with no visible sign to give it a name, and she had a feeling it was no place for a young boy, or her. "We will just—"

But her words were cut off by Taylor jumping out of the car like his ass was on fire.

"Wait," she yelled and hurried out of the car, grabbing her purse as she went.

Taylor was inside the place before she had even shut her car door. She ran after him, fearing the worst kind of debauchery to be found inside.

When she opened the door the mild chatter she'd heard coming through stopped almost immediately. The silence was so complete she heard Taylor exclaim in relief as he opened the door to the bathroom in the back and some kind of gruff rumble came from somewhere making her think there must be dogs allowed in this establishment.

"I—I'm sorry, my son had to go," she said quietly. It looked like a typical bar and grill with about thirty people drinking and eating. There was a pool table tucked in one corner with a game in progress. The people were all ages, even some kids at the tables with parents. It should have eased her mind but the way they all had frozen, as if in shock, at seeing her made her anxious. Every eye was on her now too and she wanted to back out and get in her car, but Taylor was in the bathroom. She'd never leave him unattended. She lifted her chin up with feigned confidence and walked through the crowd that had started to talk amongst themselves again. She felt hot and her heart was racing. She got to the bathroom door without incident and knocked.

"Taylor? Are you okay."

"Mom! Go away, I'm using the bathroom," he called back.

She assumed that meant he wasn't being murdered but she refused to walk away from the door.

"Why are you here?" a low growling voice asked from behind her.

Callie jumped and spun around, clutching her purse to her chest. She thought of the handgun in her glovebox and chastised herself for not grabbing it, but she'd been far too worried about Taylor walking into this place alone to think of it.

The man who'd spoken was tall and menacing. Black hair cut short and dark eyes, he was dressed in jeans and a black T-shirt that revealed full sleeves of ink on both arms and the tendrils of something crawling up the side of his neck. He had a large scar on his right cheek, and she shuddered under his accusing gaze. She felt like he hated her, despite him not knowing the first thing about her.

"My son. He's in there, I'm just waiting, he needed a pit stop," she said quietly, cringing away from him.

He frowned and narrowed his eyes at her. His nostrils flared and she wanted to cry. She turned to the door and knocked again. "Taylor, hurry up, we need to go."

"Where," the man demanded at the same time Taylor shouted.

"I'm gonna be a bit, order me a burger, I'm starving. And I want a coke."

Callie knew the man was still behind her and wished she could shrink and disappear. She wanted to become one with the wall. She pressed a hand to the bathroom door and closed her eyes, willing the tears to stay away. "N—no, we aren't staying for food."

His response was a groan and a "Please Mom, I can't eat any more granola bars and water, *please*!"

She swore she heard the man behind her growl, and she decided she didn't care if it was the men's room, she pushed her way in and quickly leaned back against the door. As if that would stop him or any other man from getting inside.

"We need to get back on the road," she reiterated, more quietly now.

"Mom, what are you doing? This is the men's room."

"And you are a boy, so I'm in here with you," she responded.

"You're so embarrassing," he mumbled from the stall.

She managed to calm herself down when no one tried to follow her into the bathroom and she ran her fingers through her blonde hair, splashed some cold water on her face and wished she could afford a shower somewhere as she used a wet paper towel to swipe at her pits. This was the way she'd been showering for four days now, and she imagined it wasn't far from losing its effectiveness.

When they left the bathroom she had a tight grip on Taylor's little hand, planning to pull him to the door and shove him in the car faster than he could argue about food.

"I heard you wanted a burger and a Coke," a waitress said as soon as they had exited the small hallway. The woman was about Callie's age and wore a black apron over tight jeans and a tank top with a logo of a wolf on it, no nametag. Her smile was friendly and her voice light.

Callie grabbed Taylor even as he was reaching for the plate on the waitress' tray. "Oh, no, we need to get back on the road," she said to the woman as well as Taylor. "We just stopped for the bathroom. I'm sorry he couldn't hold it any longer, he's just a kid."

"Understandable, you two look like you've been driving a while," the waitress said with a nod, still smiling brightly. "Well, the boss says the kid eats. If he doesn't, I throw it out," she shrugged. "I don't know about you, but I was taught never to waste food." She winked at Taylor.

Callie bit her lip and tears sprung to her eyes as Taylor wiggled to get out of her hold. The waitress leaned forward to whisper to Callie. "It's on the house, and anything you want too. We just hate to see a hungry kid and you look like you could use something substantial too, maybe a cup of coffee before hitting the road again?"

"No, I can't, I—"

"Why?" she said with a loud laugh that was friendly enough to make Callie relax a bit. "You too good for free food?"

Callie's face flamed in embarrassment, why the hell couldn't the woman have whispered that part? She felt like everyone was staring at her waiting to hear what she'd say.

"Mom! I will die if I can't eat real food today," Taylor pleaded.

Callie hated to hear how desperate her son was for a hot meal, even though she knew he was being a little dramatic. She'd gotten him a breakfast burrito that morning, but she also knew they'd been one-mealing it the last four days and he was right, granola bars weren't enough for a growing boy.

"Okay, but hurry, we do need to get back on the road."

"Heck yeah," Taylor shouted and grabbed the plate from the grinning waitress then sat at a nearby table that was empty. The families seated around them all pretended to not watch, the kids weren't very good though and a few openly stared at both Taylor and Callie. She didn't know what was going on, but she had a very uneasy feeling.

"What can I get for you? My name's Tara by the way." The waitress held out her hand. She had long black hair pulled up in a ponytail, a fresh face with just a hint of makeup over a spattering of freckles across her nose and heavy around her large black eyes. Her lips parted on a smile revealing surprisingly large teeth.

Callie shook her hand, Tara had a strong grip, but it didn't hurt, it was comforting and warm. "I'm fine," Callie said even as her stomach rumbled.

"Fucking eat something," a growling from behind her demanded, and Callie nearly folded in on herself to get away.

Tara glared at the man behind Callie then grasped her arm and led her to the table where Taylor was already sitting, mouth full of food. Callie dared a glance back and saw it was the same man who'd been outside the bathroom.

Tara gave her a soft smile as she pulled out a chair. "Don't mind Mick, he just hates to see a woman in need."

"I'm not—"

"Oh, honey," Callie watched Tara's eyes flick over the fading bruises on her cheek, "I've never seen a woman more in need than you. Sit, I'll get you a Caesar salad with some chicken and that coffee."

"I'm Callie and I would love some french fries," Callie said as she sat. If she was going to give in to this insanity she might as well indulge.

"Of course."

"Thank you."

Callie couldn't take her eyes off of Taylor as he devoured his food and when Tara brought Callie's, she also brought a slice of pie for Taylor whose eyes lit up like it was Christmas at the sight of the treat.

Callie didn't like what she was putting him through, but she knew there was no other option. If they'd stayed, she would have been killed and he would have been twisted and destroyed living alone with his father. Callie still wore the marks of the night before they'd left. She'd forgotten to buy beer at the grocery store even though that morning Oliver had told her he didn't need anything when she'd asked. Apparently, she was just supposed to know, to read his mind and predict his desires and serve them without question. He'd hit her hard, twice, and she'd fallen to the ground while he walked out of the house to get beer. When she'd looked up from where she was sprawled, doing inventory of her body, she'd seen Taylor watching from the landing, terrified and crying silent tears because he knew better than to draw his father's attention to himself.

That's when she'd known she had to get them away.

She absently touched her bruised face and lip. These people were probably staring because of the sight of her beat-up face and nothing nefarious. She just needed to relax and enjoy the meal then leave.

She ignored the rest of the room and ate slowly but her stomach was so knotted she wasn't able to get much down. Luckily Taylor was happy to finish her fries so not much was going to waste.

"Anything else for you two?" Tara asked with a cheerful smile.

"No, thank you. What do we owe?" Callie asked, nervous to hear the answer.

"Nothing. Boss said you two eat for free."

Callie didn't like that, but she wasn't going to argue because she needed every cent she had for gas to get them farther away. When Tara took the plates, Callie pulled a couple precious dollars out of her purse and left them on the table. Then she grabbed Taylor's hand and started across the restaurant.

While they'd eaten, the crowd had gone back to a loud and slightly rowdy murmur. As they moved toward the door the conversations once again stopped and she felt every eye on them. She was nervous, exhausted, and desperate to be out of the place.

MICK

"You just going to let her walk out of here?"

Mick glared at Tara. He wanted to tell his sister to mind her own damn business, her and everyone else in the room who were watching and waiting to see what he would do. But he knew she in particular wouldn't because she wasn't afraid to sass him even if he was her alpha.

"What do you want me to do? She is scared of her own shadow, has a kid in tow, and obviously is in some kind of trouble." He hadn't missed the bruises on the side of her face, the healing cut on her lip, or her bruised arm. He definitely hadn't missed the way she had clung to her purse and slunk around like a fucking mouse about to be chopped by the butcher's knife. "She is not my type."

"Oh yeah, then why has your wolf been about to crawl out of your skin ever since she walked in the door? For fuck's sake he perked up when the kid ran through as if he recognized the scent of something he was supposed to protect."

"Shut it," he growled and walked out the back door of the bar and hurried around to the front, ready to watch her get in her car and drive away. Out of his life.

His wolf was howling at the idea, it was true the wolf had taken one look at the scared woman and said '*mine*'. Too bad she had looked at him and cringed as if he was going to take his fist to her face.

"You picked wrong, you'll get over it," he said to his wolf who greatly disagreed as the woman hurried her young son into the back seat of the car and hopped in the front, locking the door immediately. "She's too scared, too broken. Do you really think she'd ever accept what we are? The violence our life seems to never be far from?"

Mick watched from his shadowy spot, but the car didn't start, it just made a noise of protest again and again as she became more frantic and frightened.

"Fuck," Mick growled and walked out of the shadow of the clubhouse. He rapped on her window as gently as he could but she still jumped, screeched, and lunged for her glovebox.

"Mom, it's just the guy from the restaurant," her son said but not before Mick caught sight of a black handgun in the open glovebox. Not only was she scared as fuck, she was armed, and that was dangerous.

The boy looked at him through the widow timidly. "Sorry sir, the car is a piece of shit," he said.

"Taylor!" Callie snapped, and her son looked appropriately chastised. Mick smiled at him though, the kid had spunk.

"Looks like you need some help," he said to her still closed door.

She shook her head and tried again but with no more luck. She dropped her head to the steering wheel and to his horror, started to cry.

"God dammit," he snarled as his wolf reached out to take control of the situation. He ripped her door open despite it being locked. He heard a gasp of surprise from her young son and was careful not to make any more sudden moves that would frighten either of them. He crouched down so his face was close to hers. "If you stop crying right now, I swear to all that is good in this universe and beyond that I will make it okay," he whispered.

She blinked and looked at him, her face wet and her plump bottom lip trembling. God she was beautiful, and so fucking fragile, what was his wolf thinking wanting to claim her? He would destroy her.

"Mom cries a lot, don't worry, it's not your fault," Taylor said from the backseat.

"She shouldn't cry, not ever," he whispered and then stood. "Okay, both of you come on, you aren't going anywhere tonight obviously. You'll stay here with us, and we can figure the rest out tomorrow. Grab what you need for a night."

"I—I—" she stammered but he reached over her and unbuckled the seatbelt.

"Just get out of the car, princess." He met her green eyes and something inside him melted. He wanted to wrap her in his arms and keep her safe for the rest of eternity. He inhaled her scent, so strong in the space where she'd spent so much time. She smelled like citrus and sunshine, his wolf wanted to roll around in it, bathe in it so that anyone who came near would know that he was claimed by this tiny fragile creature.

"Callie," she whispered but didn't move.

"Callie," he said and his wolf purred in his head. "I'm Mick. I'll have your car looked at tomorrow. For now, why don't you grab what you need. I don't think you really have any other options, and I promise you and your son are safe here."

She shook her head and gripped the steering wheel. "I don't have money for a hotel."

"Fine, because there are no hotels around here."

She looked at him with wide frightened eyes and he wondered what backwoods horrors she was imagining. She probably thought he was going to lock her in a barn at the first opportunity.

"Tara, your waitress, has an extra room. You two can stay with her tonight."

"Sure as shit they can," Tara said from behind him. He'd known she was there, along with his second in command, Lance. They'd come out as soon as he'd approached Callie's car. Probably to make sure he didn't fuck things up too bad by being overly eager or aggressive.

"Grab your things," he told her again and he watched her face as a myriad of emotions passed over it before finally it landed on acceptance. When he saw that she wasn't going to argue further, his wolf relaxed, and he felt an answering calm reverberate through the pack. No matter how they pretended not to feel what he was feeling, there was no strong emotion from the alpha that didn't spread like wildfire through the pack.

He retreated to stand with Lance as Tara helped Callie retrieve a couple small bags from the car.

"So that's her?" Lance whispered.

Mick didn't respond.

Thoughts of his mother surfaced and soured his mood. Not even the joy of watching Callie walk further into pack territory was enough to fight back the feelings that memories of his parents brought up.

Mick didn't want a human mate who wouldn't understand the power she had over him. This was why he was going to marry Janet. He didn't want or need Callie.

"You will have time to get to know her, she seems nice. Scared and delicate, but nice. You'll want to be careful with her," Lance said, watching him. "Maybe Madeline should introduce herself."

"I don't want her," Mick insisted. But even as he said it, his eyes trailed Callie as she walked with Tara and he felt his body prickle with the need to follow, to not let her out of his sight. "Fuck, I don't want a mate."

"But one just landed in your lap, Mick, what are you going to do about that?"

He didn't know. She was likely completely unaware of what

they all were and that could be an advantage. "Tell everyone that she isn't to know anything."

Lance huffed. "How long do you plan to keep her in the dark?"

"Until I'm sure I want her to know." Mick walked away from Lance and toward Tara's cabin. He told himself he just wanted to make sure she'd gotten there, but it was so much more. And the harder he tried to deny his instincts, to cling to the belief that a mate would ruin him, the more aggressively his wolf fought those thoughts and flooded him with the joy of finding their true mate.

"Fuck," he muttered as he slunk around in the shadows on the way to Tara's house. He quickly caught up to them, but kept hidden and observed her. She was in his territory, she was with not only one of his pack, but his sister, and the feelings the scene ignited in him were overwhelming and unfamiliar.

Mine. His wolf growled in his mind and Mick had no choice but to agree, and it scared the hell out of him.

Suddenly he knew he was going to have to figure out how to have her, how to keep her while maintaining his own safety. He wasn't sure he could trust her with every part of the mate bond, but maybe she didn't need to know about it.

CHAPTER 4

CALLIE

Callie had wanted to turn down the help, but she was quite literally without other options. She didn't know where the next town was or have a way to get there even if she did. Not that she had money for a hotel in a town, or money to fix whatever might be wrong with her car.

Panic threatened to strangle her. Maybe she could sell the gun or trade it for whatever her car needed. No matter what, she still had to keep moving, had to get as much space between Taylor and Oliver as possible.

She'd do whatever was necessary to keep her son safe, and at the moment she supposed that meant accepting help from these strangers. She tried to take in her surroundings as she followed Tara. It was a nice, cleared area here behind the restaurant and surrounded by trees. It looked like it used to be some kind of camp with a space for a bonfire in the middle and little cabins around. There were even trails leading back into the woods.

Tara walked to one of the cabins and Callie had to admit she was thankful that they were here, that she wouldn't be sleeping in the car again. Maybe after a decent rest she'd be clear-headed enough to make a plan.

"I will pay you back," she said to Tara as she followed her up the steps.

"For what?" Tara paused at the front door, holding it open.

Callie hesitated on the steps, holding onto Taylor so he didn't barge right in. "Letting us stay with you."

"Haven't you ever heard of helping those in need?" Tara scoffed. "Besides, if I hadn't taken you in, my brother would have, and I doubt you'd want to spend a night in that bachelor's pad."

"Your brother?"

"The big guy, Mick. He owns the clubhouse and is perpetually grumpy," Tara said with obvious adoration.

"Oh," Callie said. "Yeah." How could she not have seen it? Tara had the same eyes and mouth as Mick, definitely related.

"He's strong. Stronger than Dad. I bet he could keep you safe from Dad," Taylor said quietly. "He has tattoos!" he added as if that proved Mick's strength somehow.

Tara met Callie's eyes, her own hot with emotion and embarrassment, what would this stranger think of her? But there was only a soft understanding in Tara's gaze that made a knot in Callie's heart unravel.

Tara looked at Taylor. "Do you like ice cream, Taylor?"

"Who doesn't?"

"Mick."

"What! No way, how can someone not like ice cream? When I'm an adult I'll eat ice cream for breakfast every day because Mom won't be able to tell me no."

"Good plan," Tara said and smiled. "Come on in."

Taylor ran through the open door.

"Taylor, slow down, we are guests here," Callie called in after her son, but Tara just smiled.

"It's not a big deal. Kids are supposed to be wild. Tomorrow he'll have a bunch of friends to run around with, swim in the lake and climb trees too."

"There's a lake?" Taylor asked with excitement.

"Yep, with a big dock and a slide going into the water too. Can you swim, Taylor?"

Callie gazed around the cabin as Taylor talked Tara's ear off about his swimming lessons and the pool near their home. The interior was a small space but comfortable and tidy. The living area and kitchen consisted of one large room and there were stairs up to what she assumed was a loft bedroom. Two doors were open, showing a bathroom and a bedroom on the ground floor. A door at the back of the kitchen led outside.

"You two can use this extra room, I sleep in the loft. It's not much more than a bunk bed, but you'll be warm. And safe."

Tara's words were firm, holding a promise and even though Callie didn't know this woman, she knew Tara's words were true. At least for tonight, she and Taylor were safe for the first time in a long time.

"Thank you," she whispered, tears stinging her eyes.

Tara reached out and grasped her shoulder then turned to Taylor. "Now, I believe we were going to have ice cream."

"Only a little, he did have pie already," Callie chimed in.

Taylor was sitting at a small table, swinging his legs happily and only rolled his eyes a little at her words.

Callie loved to see her son happy, but it also made her heart twist because she knew that for all of his seven years, he hadn't been for so much of the time. It felt like her fault, she should have left sooner, she should have protected him better.

As Tara pulled out ice cream and bowls Taylor walked to the back door and peered out of the window. "Do you have a dog?"

Tara huffed a laugh. "No, but there's always a few running around, don't be afraid of them, they are all very nice."

"That one's big," Taylor said, a little fearful. He didn't have a lot of experience with animals.

Oliver hadn't let them have pets, said they were messy and useless, a lot like Callie according to him. Callie walked over to peer out into the dark. A very large dog sat staring in at them, big yellow eyes and black fur. "That's a dog?" she asked, pretty sure she was looking at something far too large.

"Wolf dog," Tara said quickly. "Don't worry, very friendly. He'd even roll over and let you rub his belly I bet."

The animal's gaze darted to Tara as if he'd heard her words and then stood and wandered off into the woods that surrounded the place.

"Where's he going?" Taylor asked.

"Probably hunting rabbits. Here's your ice cream my man, want to watch TV?"

"Yeah!" Taylor said and took the bowl to the couch, easily locating the remote and turning on the television. Kids seemed to have a sixth sense when it came to electronics, never fumbling with a new remote.

"What about you?" Tara asked, handing her a bowl.

Callie didn't want ice cream, her stomach still too unsettled by everything, but she didn't want to be rude either, so she accepted the ice cream and went to sit at the table. Tara joined her.

"You don't have to tell me your story, Callie, but if you want to, I'll listen." Tara's words were quiet and soft, tugging at something inside Callie that craved female companionship, friendship and conversation. How long had it been since she had anyone she could call a friend? Oliver had systematically cut her off from everyone without her realizing it was happening, and by the time they'd married she'd hardly been able to think of a true friend to stand beside her as bridesmaid.

Callie looked over at Taylor, happily eating ice cream and watching television in a stranger's home, and she broke down. Silent tears streamed down her cheeks, and she buried her face in her hands.

"I think you need something stronger," Tara said and motioned for her to follow.

Callie stood and Tara led her out the back door to a porch where a couple chairs sat. Tara handed her a beer she pulled from an ice chest and sat silently, waiting for Callie to talk or not.

It was her comfortable acceptance that made Callie want to open up to the stranger.

"I left my husband, I have nowhere to go, and almost no money," Callie let out a relieved laugh and took a drink of the beer. "Now apparently my car is broken too. Frick, I'm a mess." She stared down at her hands gripping the bottle, embarrassed by what she was admitting.

"Well, I think you're right on track, and I think what you did, leaving, was incredibly brave." Tara's voice broke a little and Callie darted her gaze over to the woman who was now staring intensely out into the darkness of the woods. "It took guts to abandon what little safety you had, and with your son too. But I have no doubt it was the right choice and you'll both be better off because of it."

"I stayed for years when I shouldn't have. I just kept thinking it would get better. When he got the job he wanted, when I made the right dinner, when his team won the game. Even when I told him I was pregnant for the second time." Callie's voice broke on the last and new tears came.

Tara just waited, silently supporting and it was exactly what Callie needed.

"That was three years ago. He didn't want another worthless mouth to feed, he said right before he beat me so badly I had to tell the ER nurse I was in a car accident. I lost the baby and I still stayed. I am an idiot."

"No," Tara said firmly. "You are not an idiot; you are strong, you are brave, and you are safe now."

Callie shook her head, tears running down her face. "I couldn't let Taylor see it anymore, I couldn't let him grow up thinking what his father did was okay. But I wasn't prepared to be on our own. I have no one and nothing. That's not something a smart woman does."

Tara shrugged and took another drink of her beer. The sound of a wolf howled in the distance and Callie shuddered.

"You seized a chance to escape, that is something so many wish they could do. There was no chance of your survival there, but you've given yourself and your son a real chance now, Callie. That's so brave."

Callie sighed heavily and wiped her face; she was so sick of crying about Oliver. "What the heck am I going to do now? I can't even pay for whatever's wrong with my car."

Tara perked up and smiled. "You could work at the clubhouse! I'm sure Mick would be cool with it. Stay as long as you need, earn some money for your next step and maybe *plan* a next step."

Callie wasn't sure about the idea, but did she really have a choice? She'd already taken food and shelter for free from these people, she couldn't expect to have her car fixed too. And leaving here with a little money and a plan, that would only benefit her and Taylor.

"Okay," Callie agreed. "I have a little experience. I was a server in high school for a while."

"I'm sure you'll do great."

MICK

Mick stood in the nearby woods listening to the women talk. Hearing Callie explain what she'd endured made him murderous. He wanted to run across the country and tear through the asshole's neck who had made her suffer horrors for years. Even his human instincts were screaming to avenge her and take care of her.

He calmed when he heard her agree to stay and work here for a while. It would give him the time he needed to figure out how to proceed with her.

Her son called for her from inside Tara's cabin and Callie hurried to him. Mick had no doubt that she was a great mother, and that knowledge filled him with desires to watch her mother a child of his.

Tara looked right at him, easily spotting him through the darkness of the forest.

"She's wounded," Tara said quietly.

Mick nodded his wolfy head in understanding.

"It might take a while for her to trust."

He could understand that. Trust shouldn't be easily given, and some people didn't ever deserve to have your trust. He couldn't help thinking of Janet, he didn't think he'd ever fully trust her even if they married and had kids together. He also didn't think she'd be a great mother, she seemed too selfish to give a child what it needed to thrive.

Tara went inside and Mick moved closer so he could catch glimpses of Callie as she moved through the cabin. He watched as she led Taylor to the bathroom, then into the spare room. She had to be exhausted after days of driving, he doubted she'd slept in a bed since she began her journey.

Mick shifted and walked to his own cabin, pulling on a pair of shorts he'd left on his front steps. He heard a howl nearby and some answering yips. The unmistakable sound of young wolves running, they hadn't yet learned to go like a shadow through the thick woods. It was a comforting sound for him and he hoped it wouldn't be frightening to Callie and Taylor.

How was he going to keep Callie from finding out about them before he was ready, before he thought she was ready?

"How's she settling?" Lance asked, joining him on the porch.

"She's running from an abusive husband. It sounds like she left with nothing, and has no one to help her either. Tara got her to agree to stay and work at the bar to earn money to fix whatever is going on with her car."

"You're welcome," Lance said, and Mick scowled his way. "I made sure her car wasn't going anywhere as soon as I felt what she was to you. I knew you'd need some time to settle into the idea, and I am giving it to you."

"Asshole," Mick growled but he *was* grateful. He'd been prepared to watch her drive away; to never see her again and always know she'd been within reach. All that changed as soon as she walked deeper into his territory. He was certain now he could never just let her leave even if it would be best for both of them.

Lance grinned slyly. "And I can fix it as slow as I need to."

Mick shook his head at his old friend. "I didn't want a mate."

"I know, but she's here, so what are you going to do?"

"I should let her leave but, how am I supposed to do that?

Even if my wolf wasn't desperate to claim her, she's broke and alone, in need of safety, and she has a child to care for."

"Well, you can certainly send her on her way with money, if that's what you want to do but ... if you aren't just trying to make sure she's okay when she moves on, you will need to woo her, earn her trust and learn to trust her."

"How the hell am I supposed to do that?" Mick growled.

"This is nature, you just have to let it take its course," Lance offered with a wink. "I'm sure she'll be attracted to you as well; it shouldn't be too hard. Your wolf is wired to pick a mate who is perfectly matched to both your human and wolf side. Just give her a chance to see that."

Mick couldn't help scoffing. "That didn't work out so well for my parents. What if my wolf is wrong? What if we aren't a good match?"

Lance patted Mick on the back. "I know it's hard, but you shouldn't compare what this is to what they were. They both had problems, Mick. Neither of them were right in their own selves and they made each other more wrong." Lance shrugged. "I know that sounds like it means the wolf picked the wrong mate, but I think it really just means that they were flawed and they both made choices that made it worse."

Mick grunted as Lance walked away, no doubt heading back to his family. His perfect mate and children.

Mick shifted again, knowing sleep was far off and started a route around their territory. He liked to keep an eye on his pack. The people he was dedicated to protecting and caring for. Men, women, and children whose lives depended on secrecy and the freedom to turn and run and hunt when the moon called to them.

Along with that responsibility came a link with his pack so he could better keep them safe. He could feel if they were in serious danger or stress. Tonight he could tell that they knew what he was feeling about the human in their midst, and it had them all anxious and excited, and it wasn't helping Mick feel calm at all.

Chapter 5

Kody

Kody growled as Mick passed a few feet from him. The wolf alpha didn't even stumble, just kept loping past as if he didn't care that a bigger predator was near; not that Kody would attack the wolf. He wouldn't harm anyone in Tara's pack. The problem was his brother didn't feel the same way. Kyr wanted to eliminate this threat, it was too close to their clan. Wolves and bears were natural enemies and that extended to the shifter universe.

But the shifter universe was ruled by instincts that would never occur in nature and his had claimed a pretty little wolf in that pack. It didn't make sense; no bear shifter had ever mated to anyone aside from other bear shifters and the occasional human. He wasn't even sure what would come of the union, but he knew that he was destined to be with her and no one else.

It wasn't as if he didn't know why she was hesitant. She'd seen the worst of him, and she was scared. But she wouldn't give him a chance to prove that he was trustworthy, that he would rather die than cause her any harm.

He was willing to stand against his own brother and clan for her.

"Brother," Kyr growled as he approached from behind.

Kody had heard him approaching of course, but continued to give his back to Kyr because he refused to let his brother think he was afraid. Or that just because Kyr had been born a few minutes earlier and inherited this clan, Kody would treat him like a threat. To Kody, Kyr was still the conniving whining twin brother who craved power and lost every wrestling match he didn't cheat at.

"That filthy pack is quieter than usual tonight. I'd say I'm glad you're here keeping an eye on them, but I know why you're really here and it makes me sick."

Kody didn't respond to his brother's bait, but acknowledged that it was quieter than usual. "The alpha just passed on a usual check, didn't seem agitated so I guess they're just quiet."

"Too bad, I'd love to hear they were weakened, it would be a great time to go in and send them running."

"You know I wouldn't let you do that, brother."

"You'd be better off if I did. If I got the scent of that bitch out of your nostrils."

Kody growled at his brother. "You don't need to risk the clan just because you don't want me to mate a wolf, Kyr. She doesn't want anything to do with me."

"And you don't want anything to do with any female bears because of her! We are a dying species, Kody, you have a duty to keep us alive."

"Is that why you sent Patrice over?"

"She'd be a good mate."

"So mate her," Kody scoffed.

"I have my eyes on something else."

"You mean you're waiting for the mate bond, and yet you expect me to ignore mine?"

"I expect you to do your duty to the pack," Kyr snarled and stalked off deeper into bear clan territory.

Kody stared into wolf territory; someone was staring back. It wasn't the alpha and it wasn't Tara. He nodded at the light-colored wolf and it gave a slight nod back but it didn't leave. No doubt its job was to watch him and make sure he didn't try to cross the line and get to Tara.

Didn't they understand that he'd never do anything to hurt her, that he just wanted to keep her and worship her?

The worst part was, he knew they *did* understand. But their loyalty was to Tara, their packmate, and she was hurting still. Tara couldn't trust him and so they'd stand between him and Tara until she could, if she ever did.

If only she'd give him a chance to prove himself to her. He'd wait forever if he had to of course, as if he had any other choice.

TARA

Tara relaxed on the porch and let the warm light of the moon wash over her. Callie and Taylor were asleep inside and she could sense Mick nearby, standing watch over the humans.

She didn't envy him the drama this development brought into his life, but she was thankful because it would have to change his mind from marrying Janet.

Her phone pinged with a message and before she even looked, she was sure she knew who it was. Kody often messaged her late at night, asked her to meet him, begged her for a chance.

And every time she denied him it was a little bit more difficult.

> Kyr isn't happy about Mick and Janet's marriage.

Tara was happy to alleviate that worry.

> Good thing that's probably no longer happening …

> What happened? Meet me now, we need to talk.

Tara's finger hesitated over the reply. This was important, this was about her pack and keeping it safe and so she should meet with Kody. She should explain what's going on. She didn't respond, just walked south, knowing he'd be just over the territory line. She wasn't surprised to find Serena there, staring out at Kody a few feet away.

Serena was a small white wolf, older than her, mated with four grown children. She wasn't the strongest wolf but was still capable of defending herself against Kody or any other bear if one decided to cross the border, at least long enough for backup to arrive.

"You can go home, Serena. I'll talk to him and send him on his way."

Serena gave her a slight nod with her wolf head then bared her teeth at Kody before turning and loping quietly through the woods.

Kody straightened away from the tree he'd been leaning against. His huge body loomed before her half in shadow but his face was happy, his lips turned up in a smile, and his caramel eyes were wide with hope. He had his hair pulled back in a low ponytail and she felt her body react to his attractiveness. His scent wafted toward her, cedar and musk and she bit her lip.

"Tara," he said on a breath and took a couple steps forward as if sensing her attraction.

She didn't want to give him any false hope so she held up her hand to stop him. "That's close enough, I just wanted to clarify some things. Easier to do in person."

He nodded, disappointment flashing across his face before he smoothed his features into acceptance.

"Mick met his mate tonight, a human woman. There will be no marriage to Janet and that means no union with the northern pack. Kyr can cool his shit."

"That's good but it's not going to stop Kyr. He still sees your pack as a threat too close to us. You know the best way to stop him, Tara."

Tara just shook her head because she didn't have the words to deny him. It was too hard, she felt the attraction, she felt the pull to him, and she couldn't lie. But she wasn't ready, she didn't know if she ever would be.

"Let me prove to you that I can be what you need," he begged and stepped closer.

She didn't stop him this time and he slowly closed the distance between them. He was technically in wolf territory now; she could call for an attack, it would be within her rights. But she didn't want to. She wanted to stare into his eyes and get lost there. She wanted to accept the touches he wanted so desperately to give her. She dreamed of running her fingers through his long hair.

Kody stopped in front of her and reached out slowly, his fingers traced gently along her jaw and down her neck. "Tara, you are perfection, and I would do anything to make you happy and keep you safe."

"I am safe," she whispered, unwilling to break the moment with any loud noise.

"But are you happy?"

Tara didn't have an answer to that, and she didn't move as he leaned down slowly, his lips pressing against hers in a soft kiss.

"You are my mate, Tara," he growled against her mouth.

The sound should have frightened her, but it didn't. She shivered with sudden desire as his words caressed her wolf and fed the need she'd buried deep behind fear. A soft moan escaped her lips and it seemed to spur Kody on. His hands wrapped around to her back and he crushed his lips to hers, his tongue sweeping out to demand entrance. He wasn't asking, he was dominating, and Tara loved it. She leaned into him, feeling so small against his large body.

That's when the fear trickled back in. His large hands on her back, pressing her forward, his head above her forcing her own back so he could claim her mouth, she felt surrounded. She pushed against his chest and he immediately let her go.

"I'm sorry, Kody, I can't—," her words broke and the look of calm acceptance on his face brought tears to her eyes. She was fucked up, broken, and he deserved so much better.

She turned and ran.

CHAPTER 6

CALLIE

Callie startled awake every few hours and each time tried to remember where she was as her heart hammered in her chest and her eyes darted around the dark room. When she remembered and realized she wasn't in danger, she'd peek up on the top bunk to reassure herself that Taylor was still there and sleeping, then she'd lay back down and listen to the endless sounds of wolves in the night.

Aside from her stints at summer camp she'd never been in the woods and hearing nature so close was unnerving. She wished she'd grabbed her handgun from the car just in case but, she reminded herself, Tara lived here, Mick and others lived close by as well so she had to assume she was safe from wild animals as long as she stayed in the cabin.

She managed a few hours of sleep with all the up and down. When she rose and at last saw the sun shining through the small window, she was relieved that the night was over. She had things to figure out, she had to keep moving. She couldn't do that until she had a working car, and she was going to pay for that by working at the clubhouse bar. But if she stayed too long Oliver might find them she needed to get out of here as soon as possible.

Stomach knotting with familiar fear, she peeked up at the top bunk and when she saw it was empty she was nearly overwhelmed with panic. The only thing she could think was that Oliver had found them, he had come and he'd already taken Taylor away. It was worse than him hitting her, he had torn her heart from her chest, taken her reason to live.

Gasping for air and panic constricting her chest, she burst out of the bedroom and froze.

Taylor was there, sitting on the couch with a big bowl of cereal on his lap, watching cartoons. Next to him Tara was sitting close, giggling along with the child as the cartoon animals sang and danced.

Callie let out a relieved whoosh of air.

Tara turned, giving her a wide smile. "Morning there, mama. I hope you don't mind, I only had super sugary cereal for breakfast and brain rotting cartoons on the television."

"No, I don't mind," she whispered, trying to get herself back under control.

"This is the best place ever!" Taylor exclaimed with a mouth full of cereal.

"Manners," Callie chastised.

"Sorry, Mom," Taylor said, mouth still full.

"Want some coffee?" Tara asked, walking to the kitchen.

"That would be amazing."

"Didn't sleep well?"

Callie shook her head. "I haven't slept well in ten years," she admitted.

Fury flashed through Tara's eyes before she turned to pour a cup of coffee for Callie. "Cream or sugar?"

"Yes please," Callie said.

Tara handed her the coffee with a smile. "The youngsters are itching to meet Taylor; I didn't want to send him out of the house before you were up though."

"Oh, kids live around here?" Callie said but then shook her head, she remembered Tara saying something about it last night.

"Oh yeah, this whole place is packed with families and there's always a mess of kids to play with."

"They must have heard about us having to stay the night, huh? I should find out what's wrong with my car, we need to be on our way as soon as possible." Callie felt her anxiety and panic start to ramp up again.

Tara touched her shoulder and the soft human contact soothed her so much she felt tears prickle her eyes.

"How about we sit on the front porch with coffee, you can watch Taylor play and we can chat?"

Callie could only nod, afraid her voice would start to quiver if she spoke.

"Taylor, want to meet some cool kids?"

"Yeah!" Taylor said and ran into the kitchen, dumping his bowl in the sink, then he rushed out the front door. Tara moved quickly, just a step behind the energetic boy.

Callie took a moment to collect herself before following them out, the last thing she wanted was to face anyone with teary eyes. That would invite questions. She was wearing her pajamas, leggings and an old T-shirt, feet bare and no makeup, not that she usually wore much anyway. But she felt slightly self-conscious as she stepped out into the warm morning sun and saw the crowd out there. Kids of all ages standing and staring at Tara with rapt attention as she introduced Taylor.

"This is our new friend Taylor, from the city. He doesn't know anything about being in the woods so keep him close, keep him safe."

"Is that her?" One of the older kids asked, pointing at Callie and all eyes suddenly turned her way.

"That's just my mom," Taylor said, then all the children were off running and chatting with Taylor.

Callie almost started crying again. Seeing Taylor so easily embraced by the kids and with seemingly no worries at all for what could be coming hot on their trail was everything she'd hoped to find for him.

Tara came up to sit by her.

"Thanks for doing that, he needs kids to play with. He has so much energy in him, always has," Callie said.

"As it should be with little kids, I suppose."

"Where are all their parents?" There were a couple cabins in sight of the porch all facing the cleared picnic and bonfire area but there weren't any adults to be seen.

"Some are sleeping in; some already went to work. Most are probably enjoying a moment with their mates while the kids are outside entertained," Tara said with a laugh.

"That's a lot of kids so there must be more than these seven cabins?"

"Yeah, trails lead back to other houses that are bigger. These seven and the main building with the bar and grill, were the original camp places that were here when we bought the property."

"So it *was* a camp, I knew it," Callie said feeling good about herself for a moment. "I went to a place similar in Maine when I was a kid. I spent three summers there and had a blast, best times of my life actually."

"I am sure you have good times to come," Tara said.

Callie wasn't so sure, she felt like she'd left one horrible situation and had run into another with a broken down car and no money.

"Do you think Mick really won't mind me working for a few days serving, just until I have what I need to fix the car?"

"Positive," Tara said with a bright reassuring smile.

MICK

Mick kept his distance from Callie all morning. He'd only slept a few hours, trading his patrol with Lance well after midnight. But he'd been up with the sun as usual and immediately bombarded by pack members with questions about his mate and her son. The children of the pack were particularly interested in the human boy and had gathered around Mick very early with all kinds of questions. He'd used his alpha voice, putting a power behind his words that any in his pack would be unable to go against, to swear them to secrecy about what they were and also to make them understand how important it was to keep Taylor and his mother safe while they were here. He probably hadn't needed to add the push, but he was taking no chances with Callie. Over the night he'd yearned for her and waking up knowing she was so close but not in his home had nearly driven him insane. He'd wanted to go to her, curl up in bed beside her and roll in her scent.

"Are you going to marry her and have babies with her?" a group of young girls giggled.

"Yes," he said with a confidence he didn't really feel. There was still too much to get through before he could be confident that she'd stay, that she'd be his forever.

The children had erupted in laughs and sounds of disgust then scattered, playing near Tara's home and hoping to draw the attention of Taylor.

Mick continued to watch from the shadows as Taylor scampered out to play with the kids and then Callie emerged with a cup of coffee in hand to watch. She was breathtaking in tight black pants that hugged every dip and curve of her legs and a T-shirt that was far too large and covered her to her thighs. Her blonde hair was pulled up into a messy bun and her eyes looked tired as if she hadn't slept well last night. He wanted to go to her, lead her back to bed and make her sleep. His instincts told him to protect her, heal her, and make sure she had everything she needed.

But he didn't want to overwhelm or frighten her, so he just watched.

"We have a problem," Ryland said, sliding up beside him with a serious look on his face that didn't bode well. He was an older member of the pack and a trusted advisor to Mick.

"I don't have time for problems," Mick snarled, watching as Taylor joined the kids in a game of soccer in the clearing.

Ryland grunted and shook his head; he wasn't scared of Mick's anger. "You'll want to handle this sooner rather than later, trust me."

Mick did trust Ryland, so he gave up his view of Callie and Taylor to follow Ryland to the clubhouse. Mick's stomach dropped when he scented her before he even entered the room and saw her waiting like a coiled snake to poison the future he'd just been dreaming about.

"Micky! Babe!" Janet squealed and jumped at him, wrapping her arms around his neck and pressing her too skinny body against his in a way he knew she expected would elicit an erotic reaction. She pressed kisses to his cheek and her scent filled his nostrils, turning his stomach even more. She smelled like vanilla and a cloying musk of a pack that wasn't his. He pushed her away a little too roughly, gaining a frown from her and a slight growl from

Royal. She expected to attract him; to have him panting and ready to breed, but all he could think about was that this wasn't the tiny human who was his mate, and it felt wrong to have her so intimately near him. Callie smelled like citrus and sunshine and a musk that was so soft and unique to her that he'd never be able to describe it, and he wanted no substitute. Janet was dressed to entice him in short, cutoff shorts barely covering her ass and a tiny tank top that clearly showed she wasn't wearing a bra. Her large breasts popped out the top and her hard nipples pressed against the fabric indicating she was feeling ready for him despite the lack of a mate bond. She was wearing heavy makeup, her eyes lined in thick black and her lips were painted a deep red.

It was so fake, Mick almost laughed in her face. Did she really think this false appearance was going to win him over?

Once upon a time he'd found her attractive enough of course, but now all he felt was repulsion as she preened in front of him.

Oh how his plans had been blown to dust the moment Callie had chased her young son into the clubhouse. Now with this female in front of him the reality hit that he'd never be able to be with anyone but Callie. If she left, if she didn't accept him, or if he decided it was too risky and he sent her away, he'd never have another woman because the disgust his wolf was filling him with at the thought was so overwhelming he knew he'd never be able to get past it.

He was doomed to have no one if not Callie.

Janet was pouting at him as he scowled, making him want to roll his eyes, but he ignored her and turned to the real problem.

Her father's blue eyes were flickering slightly yellow showing he was on edge being in another alpha's domain and no doubt sensing that something had changed.

"I have to call it off," Mick said, not bothering to sugar coat anything.

Janet let out a vicious growl and Royal glared at him, his eyes turning fully yellow as his wolf started to surface with his anger.

Mick felt his own wolf start to surface but knew the last thing he wanted was this interaction to turn into a physical fight, especially with Callie and Taylor so close and vulnerable. He pushed his wolf back and took a breath, knowing that calm reason was what would work here.

"We had a deal, Mick. You are marrying Janet, and I am protecting you from the bear clan."

He nodded. "Yes, but that was before I found my mate. You know I can't marry Janet now. With no commitment in place to keep my wolf from attaching, I can't ignore the draw to her."

"What the fuck? You've sniffed every female in a hundred mile radius, you don't have a mate and neither do I," Janet snarled. "This was a done deal, Mick. You don't even want a mate," she added with a snarl.

Mick hated what he had to tell them next. It was exposing a serious vulnerability. "You're right, I didn't, but that didn't stop it from landing on my doorstep, and besides, she isn't a wolf," Mick gritted. He needed Royal to understand the delicacy of the situation and why he wasn't about to bring out the woman and prove there was a mate bond, because technically there wasn't yet, not until he bit her and set it, something that would have been done almost immediately if she'd been a wolf shifter too.

Janet pouted, "Daddy!" she demanded then stomped a foot and growled. "This is unacceptable, I won't be put aside for a fucking human. Where is she? I'll rip her—"

Mick moved fast, he had his hand around Janet's throat and her back pressed against a wall in seconds. "She's more than a human, she's my *mate*, so watch your mouth."

Janet's eyes were bright yellow, and her body rippled beneath his hold. Mick forced her change to stop with his own demanding gaze, his wolf coming out to control hers, shifting his jaw and teeth, yellowing his eyes and stretching his ears. He knew he would look terrifying but most importantly, he was dominating. Her wolf was weak, Mick could see that clearly now no matter how she hid it behind bravado and snark. It was likely why Royal was trying to marry her off outside his own pack, and she submitted to Mick easily.

She dropped her gaze and whined. Mick backed away from her and faced Royal, his facial features back to normal but his eyes still slightly yellow.

"You know I wouldn't have backed out of the deal if it wasn't for this unexpected and unwanted change. I hope we can still find a way to work together. It just won't be through this marriage," he said motioning between himself and Janet.

"I see that," Royal said stiffly and snapped his fingers at his daughter who was no longer cowering but glaring at her father as if she had expected him to fight harder for her.

She stormed out of the bar and once the door closed behind her, Royal turned to Mick. "I understand you found your mate and have no choice but to claim her, but I won't offer protection without allegiance. I still need that girl off my hands," he growled the last.

Mick nodded understanding. "I hope we can find another way to live peacefully here."

Royal turned and left without another word.

As the clubhouse door swung open, Mick heard a voice that made his heart skip and when he realized she was talking to Janet, he groaned. This was not how he wanted to first interact with Callie today.

He hurried out to the front porch and saw Callie standing by her car, arms wrapped around herself in a defensive position. Tara was behind Callie with a worried look on her face, she glanced at Mick as if she wanted him to tell her it was okay to attack Janet, but he couldn't, not without cause.

Mick glanced from Janet to Callie, there was no comparison between the two women. He didn't want what Janet could give him. Even before Callie had entered the clubhouse last night he'd known that Janet was only a means to an end, not a desired mate.

He felt dirty for ever touching the woman and when Janet looked his way, he saw the moment that knowledge filled her, and he saw a vulgar desire there.

Before he could stop her, Janet was speaking words that he was certain would drive Callie as far from him as possible.

"Good luck with that violent asshole," Janet said, touching the slight redness around her neck where Mick had pressed. "Broke our engagement with no reason and after he already fucked me too, apparently that's all he wanted."

"You bitch!" Tara growled and made a jump for Janet.

Mick couldn't move. He wanted to stop the horror that was running over Callie's features and the waves of fear that were quivering through her body, and he knew he needed to stop Tara from making a deadly mistake. But he could do neither for what felt like an eternity as he watched his chance at a happy future dissipate with Janet's words.

Ryland was thankfully near the women and quick to react, and so was Royal. They each grabbed a girl and pulled. Janet played it up and turned into her father's embrace, crying against his chest about the horribly violent people who lived here as he led her to the waiting truck.

Tara ripped herself out of Ryland's hold and went straight to Callie who looked about to bolt.

Lance ran around the clubhouse ready to deal with whatever had just rippled through the pack. No doubt Mick's anger and fear, mixed with the rage in Tara, had set everyone on edge.

Mick stepped forward, finally able to move through his fear of having everything fucked up so soon.

Tara was trying to reassure Callie who was staring at the departing vehicle that held Royal and a tearful Janet. "Don't listen to that trash, come on. I'll show you what we can prep in the kitchen for lunch."

"I should just go check on Taylor," Callie whispered and fled back toward the cabins without even a glance in Mick's direction.

Tara glared at Mick. "What the fuck?"

"I didn't know she was coming today, or at least I forgot she was coming today," he admitted.

"You may have just lost your chance at your mate, brother."

He didn't respond because he knew she was right and a part of him, the scared child part of him, thought it was probably for the best. His wolf growled in hearty disagreement.

Mick was trying to decide if he should go after her when Lance grabbed his arm and shook his head. "Give it a minute, Mick. She's not going anywhere, remember, not until I fix her car. Let her settle down, then talk to her straight, explain some things when she's calm and ready to listen."

Mick nodded and walked to his bike. He needed to calm down too and he needed to think. Neither of those things were possible this close to her. He started the bike and took off down the road confident that his pack would keep her safe for him.

CHAPTER 7

CALLIE

Callie wasn't okay, she wasn't calm, and she didn't feel safe. She'd been more than a little triggered by the red marks on the woman's neck and the implication that Mick had put them there, it tore away the sense of safety she'd started to carefully accept. She didn't know what to do now, could she stay here if he had done that? Did she even have a choice? She still didn't have a car. Could she just avoid him until it was fixed though?

She made it back to Tara's cabin and went inside to start grabbing the few things they'd brought from the car. She was heading back to the door to find Taylor and maybe start walking, hopefully toward a town, when Tara appeared in the doorway, arms crossed over her chest, and with a raised eyebrow.

"It's not what you think."

"I saw the marks on her neck. After what I told you, do you really think I can stay here? Work for him?" Callie felt frantic and her voice cracked with emotion.

Tara's face softened in sympathy. "Do you trust me?"

"Yes, but you're not the only one here and I just ... I just can't let Taylor see that from someone else, I wanted to keep him away from it."

"I understand, but I need to show you something before you make a decision. Come with me," Tara said and turned around. "Leave the bags."

Callie was sure she was being naïve, but she did as Tara instructed. She dropped the bags on the couch and followed her outside. Tara was halfway across the clearing already and Callie hurried to catch up.

"Where did all the kids go?"

"They are around somewhere, safe, don't worry, they know how to take care of each other here."

Callie wasn't completely reassured by that; she'd like to set eyes on Taylor at least. But she *did* trust Tara, so she kept following the woman.

Tara didn't stop at the edge of the clearing, just continued down a path that led into the woods and after a few minutes stopped at the edge of a yard. The house that rose up on the other side of it was much larger than the cabins, looked to be two stories, probably five bedrooms at least. On the porch stood a very pregnant woman fanning herself with a magazine as she watched three kids wrestle around in a sprinkler on the lawn.

"That's Madeline. She's pregnant with her fourth kid, her husband is Lance, you saw him earlier, he's the one who's going to fix your car by the way. She's known me and Mick since we were all kids together, she even dated Mick for a while in high school, they broke up when she decided she was destined to marry Lance. Lance is Mick's best friend, been married to Madeline for ten years now. Do you think that any woman in her right mind would not only marry the best friend of an abuser she'd dated, but would continue to raise her kids in the same community as him, with him being the one in charge of all this?"

Callie didn't know what to say, she'd stayed with her abuser for ten years, who's to say what she would have done in Madeline's situation. Honestly, who's to say Lance wasn't abusive and controlling, Madeline certainly would have a hard time leaving and taking so many kids, especially while pregnant.

Tara gave a frustrated huff. "Still skeptical? Okay, come on." She strode forward across the lawn and waved at the woman "Hey, Madeline, how the hell are you standing? You look like you're as big as a whale."

"Fuck you, Tara. I—" she froze, her eyes landing on Callie who was slowly following. "Shit a brick, is that her?"

Callie looked behind her, assuming she'd be talking about someone else, but there was no one. She looked back at Madeline who was grinning at her with a wide smile now. "I met your boy earlier, he came through with the other kids when things started to feel tense. But then they headed out again since it's calm, they're making sure he feels welcome and safe. Sorry I didn't make it out yet to introduce myself but as you can see." She waved a hand from her large belly to the laughing children. "I have my hands full and I'm tired as fuck."

Callie felt like she was missing something, not understanding everything Madeline had implied. "Oh, no worries, I mean, no need to introduce yourself to me. I hope Taylor was polite when he came by though," Callie said, a little uncomfortable with the woman's friendliness.

"Very polite," she agreed, "Come sit, I'll get some iced tea. I'm off coffee, sorry."

"Oh no, don't trouble yourself, I'm fine," Callie said, not wanting this poor woman to have to do anything, she looked like she could squat and push out that baby any second.

"I'll get it, you tell Callie about dating Mick," Tara said dryly and walked into the house.

"Oh Mick, what a sweetheart," Madeline gushed. "It's too bad he wasn't the one for me but when I saw Lance one day it was like a lightning bolt from my groin straight to my heart," she laughed.

"You were dating Mick and left him for Lance?" Callie couldn't imagine that going well.

"I did, guy took it well, he knew we weren't meant for each other. It's a kid thing, trying people out even though you know it isn't forever. I'm sure you did the same. A pretty girl like you likely dated all through school, breaking hearts." Her smile was genuine and nonjudgmental, it relaxed Callie a bit.

"I guess so ..." Callie said but she couldn't really relate, Oliver was the only man she'd ever been serious with.

"Well, anyway all that's over now, huh? No more playing the field for us."

"Yeah, you seem to be pretty tied down to Lance," Callie agreed with a laugh, ignoring the insinuation that she was in the same situation.

"No, I mean with—" she stopped and seemed to remember herself. "Well I just mean things change. Sometimes the right man walks through the door and fucks up everything we thought we knew about life and love."

Tara emerged from the house then, thankfully keeping Callie from having to respond to that. She had three glasses of iced tea and handed them around. They spent the next hour talking and Callie felt so at ease she almost forgot that she'd been about to flee, possibly hitchhike to get away from the possible danger of Mick.

When Lance showed up covered in grease head to toe and leaned in for a kiss from his wife she snarled and threatened his next meal if he so much as touched her while he was so dirty.

Callie stiffened, braced herself to see a reaction that would no doubt embarrass and possibly harm Madeline. But it didn't come. Lance straightened and blew his wife a kiss then walked inside saying he'd be in the shower if she needed him.

"Wow, Callie you're white as a ghost, are you alright?" Madeline asked a little panic in her voice. "Tara is she okay?"

"Yeah, she's okay," Tara said and put a hand on Callie.

Callie looked at Tara with wide eyes and saw an understanding there that made her relax slightly, she took a shuddering breath, and she accepted that Lance wasn't Oliver, that Madeline wasn't afraid, and maybe, she was safe here too.

Maybe.

A few minutes later Madeline told her kids to go off and play with their friends then stood. "Well, pregnancy makes me horny, so I'm going to join Lance in the shower, he should be mostly clean by now," she laughed.

Tara laughed as well and Callie's cheeks flamed. "Thanks for the tea," she said and followed Tara back across the yard.

"I know what you were trying to show me, but I also know what I saw, Tara. You can't even begin to understand what I've been through."

Tara stopped in the middle of the woods, the light filtering through the trees gave her an eerie sort of glow and Callie was once again wrapping her arms around herself. Tara lifted her shirt and Callie gasped. There was a long, jagged scar running from just under her right breast to her belly button. It looked old but was still purple and angry. It had to have nearly killed her.

"I was in love with a guy I worked with at Denny's," Tara explained, putting her shirt back down. "Allen was a line cook. I moved in with him even though Mick didn't approve and tried to tell me Allen was trouble. I thought I knew him better." Tara rolled her eyes and sighed. "The first time he hit me he looked so surprised I immediately forgave him. The second time, he told me it was my fault and I believed him. I had come home late, and he hadn't known where I was." She lifted her shirt slightly this time, just showing the edge of the scar. "When he did this, it was because my brother had come into the restaurant and demanded that Allen let me come home for a family party. It was an overnight thing and Allen wasn't invited. I wanted to go too but Allen heartily disapproved of me spending any time away from him, certainly not overnight with my family. As soon as Mick left the restaurant Kody waltzed in. He lives south of here and has a sort of crush on me, thinks we are destined to be together. He was spouting his usual shit about me being his soulmate and the two things were enough to really set Allen off. He caught me in the hallway and used a kitchen knife to almost kill me. If Kody hadn't been there, I might have died that day." Tara smoothed her shirt down. "I get it, and I would never let a man abuse a woman around me, but if Mick put his hands on that dumb whore, Janet, you better believe it kept them both safe in the situation *she* put them in. There's a lot of shit you don't know. Try not to judge Mick and the rest of us based off of your horrible experience. Trust us, and you *will* heal here, Callie, I know you will."

Callie didn't know what to say. She burst into tears and embraced Tara. "I am so sorry that happened to you."

"Thank you, I hope it helps you to understand that I would never let you be in a situation that could get you hurt. I'd never stand by my brother if he was abusive. I know that's not him though, and I know that Janet bitch would gladly scratch all our eyes out to get what she wants."

Callie nodded and pulled away, wiping her tears. She understood what Tara was trying to do and she did appreciate it, but in the end, she still didn't trust Mick. Although between Madeline and Tara's reassurance, she'd changed her mind about hitchhiking away with Taylor at least.

"Okay, let's go get the prep done so we can open the clubhouse before people start wanting lunch."

MICK

Mick didn't return to the clubhouse until the sun was close to setting. As soon as he was off his bike, Lance and Madeline walked up to him. Well, Lance walked and Madeline had a sort of waddle to her usually smooth gait.

"I met your girl this morning. Pretty thing, awfully scared though," Madeline frowned at him. "I had to tell her what a nice guy you are."

"Thanks, do you think it helped? Do you think she feels safe here?"

He would die keeping her safe and so would the pack; that's what it meant to be mated to the alpha. Except they weren't mated, not officially and his wolf liked to keep reminding him of that.

Madeline snorted. "You could tell her what's going on, I think that would go a long way to making her feel safe."

"She's a human, she needs to understand a hell of a lot before I throw in the fact that my wolf has decided he wants to keep her."

"So tell her what she needs to know to convince her that staying is the best option for her and Taylor. Let her get to know you, trust will come."

"I'm not sure how to do that," Mick grunted.

"Well, I'm not sure being gone all day fighting with bears was a great way to do that," she said with narrow eyes, sniffing in his direction.

Mick had decided he needed to work off his frustrations and the easiest way away from his pack to do that was to go through neutral human territory and up to the western edge of the bears'. It'd been easy to find a fair fight there and he'd walked away with a couple scratches and a comforting exhaustion.

Now that he was back and he could smell that Callie was just inside the clubhouse, all of that relaxation was replaced by nervous energy and the need to claim what his wolf had decided was his.

"Be gentle with her," Madeline said, reaching out to touch him and he felt his wolf settle. She had that effect; she was an omega. It was her natural ability to calm those around her that had first led him to date her in high school. Too bad she wasn't his mate, a fact he'd been grateful for up until now. It would have been easier with her, but he was glad she'd ended up with someone like Lance, he was the best man Mick knew.

"I know," Mick snarled. "My only goal right now is to make her trust me enough so that I can reveal what we are without her completely losing her mind." One thing he'd decided while away that day was that he wanted her to know. Whether she stayed or not, whether she accepted him or not, he wanted her to know what he was, what they were, what was out there. It felt dangerous for her not to know because obviously there was something in her that was attractive to a wolf. He feared other wolves would sense it and want to claim her too. There wouldn't be a mate bond with another wolf, but there could still be a desire for a relationship.

The thought of her falling into the arms of another male made his stomach churn and his wolf howl. He'd never be able to watch her with someone else, human or wolf, it would kill him.

Madeline smiled brightly and touched his cheek again. "You

are a good man, Mick, and she's lucky to have you. Now, Lance, take me home, I need to put my feet up."

Mick watched Lance help his very pregnant mate home and ached for that. He had never let himself hope for what they seemed to have, had taken it out of the equation for his future because it felt too risky to have a mate, to give someone else that kind of control, but now ... now it was right in front of him, and it still terrified him, but he also wanted it, badly.

How the hell was he going to get Callie to trust him? That needed to come first, then he'd decide how *much* he could trust her with.

Mick walked into the clubhouse not at all surprised to see it absolutely packed tonight. It seemed everyone in the pack had decided on dinner out for the chance to catch a glimpse of his mate. They all turned eyes on him as he walked in, some obvious and some subtle. But he didn't care about the curious eyes, he cared about the woman who was currently taking orders. She had changed into some long jean shorts and a black T-shirt with an apron over it. Her hair was in a high ponytail, and she'd put on some makeup covering most of the bruising that had still been prominent even this morning.

Just remembering seeing it there made him clench his fists and a couple teenagers at a nearby table growled, feeling his anger. He gave them a firm look and they quieted down, they were young, just learning how to control their wolves and the influx of alpha emotions affected them more than the adults.

She hadn't spotted him yet, so he walked to the bar where Tara was standing glaring at him. He sat on a stool and she snapped. "Where the hell have you b—oh, never mind, I smell it on you. Bears."

There was a hint of worry in her voice that he knew had nothing to do with himself since he was obviously fine sitting in front of her.

"Really, Mick, you thought you could fight her out of your system?"

"Don't worry it wasn't Kody."

She relaxed slightly no matter how she tried to hide it and raised an eyebrow.

"No, I thought I could calm myself enough to not prove her right."

Tara's face softened and she tilted her head at him. "You would never harm her or anyone else unless it was necessary."

"No, but I would drag her to my cabin and never let her out again even if she hated me for it."

Tara laughed and he didn't appreciate it at all. "As soon as she told you to let her out you would, and you know it. The bond is going to give that tiny human control over your wolf and that's the part that terrifies you." She gave him a serious look. "She's sweet and delicate and as far as I can remember, nothing like our mother, Mick. I don't think you have anything to be afraid of."

"Beer," he growled, and she complied.

"She's doing well, we visited Madeline and that really calmed Callie down. I even told her about Allen so she'd understand I would never put someone in danger like that. She's been working hard all day, determined to make enough money to pay for her car and skip out of here as soon as possible."

Mick wasn't surprised but he hated to hear it.

"Where's Taylor?"

"I have Tiffany and Sarah babysitting him at my place. They have decided that since they are babysitting the alpha's stepson they are basically the most important teens in the pack and in charge of all the other kids," she said rolling her eyes.

Mick smiled at that, those two pre-teen girls were a handful, the last thing they needed was something to lord over the other kids in the pack. But hearing that the pack kids had accepted Taylor to such a degree warmed him more than he could have imagined. He drank his beer and watched Callie through the mirror at the back of the bar. He was aware of her everywhere she went, and she seemed to be doing everything she could to avoid him.

But that told him one important thing, she was aware of him too.

As he sat and watched her, pack members came to talk and congratulate him and offer dating advice. None of which he planned to use. After a while he couldn't take it anymore and retreated to his office in the back. Which is where Callie finally decided to face him.

The knock was almost too quiet to hear, and he knew it would be her walking in when he said enter.

She stood just inside the doorway not letting it close her in and crossed her arms protectively over her chest. She looked tired but also there was an air to her that he hadn't seen last night. Accomplishment, he thought, and wondered if she'd ever been allowed to have a job. Many abusive and controlling men didn't allow their women to work, wanted them home all the time where they could control almost every aspect of their lives. He felt proud to know he'd given her this. It was something that was hers, an ability to accomplish and earn and feel powerful even in a small way.

"Callie, I hope you had a good first day."

"What are you planning to pay me and how much will fixing my car take?" she asked, ignoring pleasantries.

Mick fisted his hands under his desk, why did she have to want to get away? Where the hell was she even going to go?

Nowhere, that's where.

"I'll have to talk to Lance, he's the mechanic around here and I think he has to order a part from town tomorrow, could take a few days to get it in."

She took a step back, her eyes going to the ground in front of her and her body folding slightly in on itself as if she were trying to make herself a smaller target. "Umm, okay, yeah that makes sense.

I'm sorry, I don't want to be a problem I don't mean to overstay. I'm sorry I—"

"Stop," he growled and instantly regretted it. He couldn't stand to hear her cower and beg forgiveness like that. She should never beg anyone for anything, she should never apologize for simply existing.

She stepped back again so she was fully in the hall now and looked around as if hoping to find someone else close by to witness whatever violence she imagined he was about to heap upon her.

Mick took a breath and closed his eyes. "Callie, you are not to apologize for being here, you are not to worry about a damn thing. Just, just, ah fuck. I don't know just relax, okay?"

"Sure, sorry," she said again and bit her lip, her eyes downcast as she took another step away from him, her back almost against the wall now.

He looked at her and he knew his eyes were probably halfway to yellow and he was glad she refused to meet them. His instincts roared at him to comfort her so he stood, intending to do just that but the scrape of his chair had her running before he could say or do anything to make the situation better.

Two minutes later Tara was in his doorway glaring. "Could you stop sending her crying from the clubhouse?"

Mick rubbed his face and growled. "I am trying!"

"Try harder," she growled back and left, slamming his door as she went.

He was fucking it up, he knew it and not just for himself. His whole pack was invested in this relationship working because if a pack's alpha was distracted by a mate's rejection. He wasn't strong enough to keep them all safe. Making Callie trust him was more than about him having his mate, it was what the pack needed, especially now that he had cut the tentative tie with the north pack. The bears to the south were restless, unpredictable, and as eager as ever to take over the territory of Mick's relatively small pack. He knew that one of the only reasons they hadn't yet was because of Kody.

Kody, pining away at their border for Tara. He was a sad sight, and Mick knew he was looking just as sad, himself, at the moment.

Mick had to get his shit together. He was alpha, and his duty was to the pack. He would do anything to keep them safe and right now that meant convincing Callie that she could trust him.

CALLIE

Callie forced herself to stop and take some deep breaths before she reached Tara's cabin. She didn't want Taylor to see her like this and she didn't want his sweet babysitters to either. She counted to fifty then started walking at a casual pace.

She'd half expected Mick to follow her as she'd fled his office. She wasn't sure why there was a slight disappointment that he'd just let her go. As if his non-reaction was proof he really did only see her as an annoyance in his space. She had no right to want him to see her as anything else.

A noise in the nearby woods had her increasing her pace. No matter what Tara had said about the wildlife around here; she was still nervous about the number of howls she'd heard last night.

"Callie, we fed him and watched a movie, we played a game and had him shower then put him to bed," one of the preteens, Tiffany, started babbling as soon as Callie walked into the cabin.

"I read him a story and made sure he brushed his teeth!" the other girl, Sarah, added enthusiastically.

Callie smiled at the two girls, so sweet and eager to please. She pulled out most of the tips she'd collected during the dinner rush and handed it to them. They giggled and ran out with promises of babysitting any time she needed.

Feeling settled, Callie checked on Taylor, got ready for bed, and stared out the window at the darkness while her mind replayed the day.

It had started okay, there was a definite trip up early on she still wasn't sure how she felt about … but working had been wonderful. She hadn't realized how badly she'd needed something to do, something to make her feel capable, as if she had a real chance at taking care of Taylor and herself.

She wondered if Mick would let her use him as a job reference when she left. It would help her get hired when she eventually found somewhere safe to stay a while.

What would a safe place be like? she wondered.

This place felt safe, surrounded by people who didn't know Oliver. Far from the bustle of a city, she liked that, and nature was calming. But she couldn't stay in Tara's tiny cabin forever and there didn't seem to be any empty houses around. She wasn't even close to being able to afford to build a home here, so that meant she needed to move on when possible. This was okay, for now, but it wasn't their permanent stop.

A howl ripped through the night reminding her that there were things about this place she certainly didn't like.

That night she dreamed of Oliver. He'd found them, he held a knife to her throat and sneered down at her in the dark.

She woke with a scream, Taylor shaking her with his small hands, his face twisted in worry.

"Mom, Mom, it's just a dream," he was saying.

She grabbed him and held him so tight he grumbled in complaint but let her have her moment. When she let go, he offered to get her some water but she sent him back to bed and got it herself.

Staring out the kitchen window she was surprised to see a large black dog. Was it the same one she'd seen yesterday when they'd first arrived here at Tara's cabin? She supposed that meant it was friendly but the way it looked directly at her made her shiver and she hurried back to bed.

"We're safe here aren't we? I don't worry about you here," Taylor whispered as Callie snuggled back under her blankets.

Her heart broke and her voice shook when she answered. "You shouldn't ever have to worry about me, it's my job to do the worrying."

"Tiffany and Sarah said that Mick would keep us safe here because he's in charge and no one is stronger than him."

Callie rolled her eyes in the dark at the teenage idealization. "We are safe, go to sleep, Taylor." What was it with everyone and Mick? He was obviously respected here, was it some kind of gang? They did have a lot of motorcycles and she'd thought when they first pulled up to the place that it was a biker bar they were walking into.

Or was it some kind of cult? The thought was sobering, had she accidentally led her son into the heart of some religious fanatic's commune?

She needed to ask a few pointed questions tomorrow, she didn't want to be forced to drink any kool-aid or become someone's tenth wife, even if it was being offered by a big, sexy, powerful—she stopped herself from continuing those thoughts. The attractiveness of Mick didn't make him safe.

"Can we stay?" Taylor asked.

"For a while, baby, now go back to sleep."

Thankfully the rest of the night was dreamless.

CHAPTER 8

TARA

Tara hadn't been asleep when she heard Callie's nightmare shake her awake. She'd been about to go check on her when she heard Taylor taking care of his mother, what a strong child he was. He'd seen so much, and deserved to be a kid, Tara hoped he'd get that here.

She listened to the sound of Callie getting water and heading back to bed, and then the cabin was quiet once again. She rolled over with a sigh and grabbed her phone; the reason she'd already been awake. She wanted to call Kody. She wanted to make sure he was okay. Even if Mick said he hadn't attacked Kody, he'd gotten in a fight with one of the bear shifters. She needed to be certain that Mick didn't do anything to damage the tentative stalemate they were in with the clan to the south.

Yes! She told herself, that was reasonable.

She took her phone and walked out of the cabin silently. She didn't stop until she was all the way past the clubhouse and to the road so she'd have some privacy and dialed Kody.

"Tara," Kody answered on the second ring.

She was frozen for a moment, his voice sliding over her like a caress, and she had to close her eyes, her hand clenched around the phone.

"Tara, are you okay?" Kody asked, a little frantic this time.

"Yeah," she managed. "Yeah, I was just calling because Mick went and got in a fight. I wanted to make sure he didn't hurt anyone."

"Your brother and Spencer went at it on the border to the west. I guess they both talked first, set some rules then wrestled around and got in a few punches. Spencer came back with a grin because he got to hit the alpha, but no one was bleeding."

Tara was relieved. "So he didn't incite a war, that's good."

"Kyr is pissed, he'd take any excuse to attack the pack, Tara. I don't know how much longer he'll wait. If you'd just accept that we can fix things ..."

Tara gritted her teeth, images of Kody filling her mind, his strong body, his handsome face, and then, his large teeth, blood covering him after attacking Allen. His vicious growls, the murder in his eyes.

She shivered. "Kody, I don't want you," she snapped. "You have to accept that, but I do appreciate you not letting your psychotic brother attack my pack."

She hung up the phone and when it rang back with Kody's name lighting up the screen she hit ignore and shoved it in her pocket.

"Fuck!" she yelled.

"You're setting this pack up for quite the fight, Tara," David said, startling her.

Tara turned and found him leaning against a tree, glaring at her. There was always someone awake, someone wandering, someone keeping watch. She shouldn't have thought she could actually have some privacy despite the time.

"I'm not the sacrificial lamb, David," she snarled back.

"No, you're the selfish wolf. Your brother was willing to marry a random bitch to keep us safe, you aren't willing to marry your mate," he scoffed.

"He's not my mate."

"Isn't he?" David snarled back and then turned and walked into the woods.

Tara felt her phone vibrate and she pulled it out to see a text from Kody.

I want to talk to you. I want to see you.

Tara's fingers hovered over the reply button, but she turned it off instead and stuffed it back into her pocket. Perhaps the most dangerous thing about Kody was that she wanted to trust him, she wanted to lose herself in his arms. But could she ever trust him despite what she knew he was capable of?

KODY

Kody glared down at his phone. No ellipsis, no response, and it made him want to tear his way across the forest and force her to face him. Not that an action like that would help his case with her, she was already afraid of his physical power.

His hands fisted as he remembered. How he'd gone absolutely insane in those moments when she was bleeding. He'd lost every ounce of humanity and control and his bear had torn through that human like he was nothing.

It would have been better perhaps if he'd shifted, but he'd done it in his mostly human form and that seemed to add to Tara's fear. When she looked at him, she said she could only see the horror that he'd inflicted, deserved or not.

"They attacked without provocation; this shit has to stop!" Kyr was growling, pacing around the living room and making sure that everyone gathered was listening.

Kody stepped back into the house.

This was a meeting of the elders. He and Kyr were the ruling family of the clan but there were elders who were respected and who they went to for input. Four of them sat around looking thoughtful. Samuel, Gregory, Patty, and Franklin. All too old to contribute to the clan in any way other than knowledge, they'd earned their place as respected elders and were well taken care of by the younger members. However, those younger members' numbers had dwindled in the last fifty years and with no close by clans of bear shifters to unite with, they struggled with what the future might hold for them. They'd been here for over five hundred years, ruling this southern forest of Idaho. None of them wanted to see that come to an end.

"I have a possible mate coming in from Alaska and I don't plan to have her be in the middle of a war. We need to end this," Kyr snarled.

That was a new bit of news to Kody and he sent a suspicious look towards his brother. When was Kyr planning to share that information with him? Inviting a single bear into the clan was a big deal, for all unmated bears. He wondered if the poor girl knew what she was walking into.

"We've always lived peacefully next to the wolves," Patty pointed out, always the most reasonable of the elders.

"Those dogs are lucky we've let them live near this long. I say take them out, we need space for the children Kyr and Kody will bring us," Gregory growled.

Kody met Kyr's gaze across the room, his brother giving him a narrowed look with a lip twisted up. A silent threat no doubt, Kyr didn't want Kody to start talking about who he wanted to start making babies with.

Kody turned back to the elders. "Spencer entered into a fair match willingly with rules of no major injuries. Mick respected that, it was just a wrestling match, nothing more, just blowing off steam," Kody argued.

"He was testing our strength, learning what we are capable of, don't you see the trick he's playing? We need to attack sooner rather than later," Gregory argued.

The other two elders remained silent, nodding at what everyone said and taking no side. Kody could see he was going to have no allies here. He bared his teeth at Kyr and stormed out of the house. He would fix this. He would do what he needed to do in order to make sure that Tara and her pack were safe.

Kody pulled out his phone and pressed on a name he regretted having in his phone.

"Kody," Janet's seductive voice answered almost immediately. "It's a pleasure to finally get a call, big boy. You miss me?"

He didn't, he regretted her more than anything he'd ever done in his life. But he needed her help now.

"I need to know what you know about Mick and his pack. There's a human there, what's the full story? I thought you two were getting hitched soon."

He could hear the pout in her breath as she huffed into the phone. "That's a lot of questions and I'm hungry, take me out."

The last thing Kody wanted to do was get close to that viper of a woman again, but he knew she wasn't going to answer his questions any other way. "Fine."

Chapter 9

Callie

Callie was sitting on Tara's porch drinking coffee and watching Taylor talk with a few kids. The morning was already warm and she felt like she'd slept better than she had in years, despite the nightmare. She was so frustrated, mostly at herself. She didn't used to be this girl; this frightened apologizing female. She used to be strong. She was head cheerleader, and she'd worked her way through high school at a local restaurant with a smile and a confident swagger that had always made good tips. She'd gotten straight A's in school and even took the harder classes because she'd had plans.

Plans that went out the window when Oliver told her she was best suited to stay home while he worked on his career. He'd undermined her confidence, taken away her choices, her friends, and her opportunities. In fact, she was sure that the only reason he'd gotten her pregnant with Taylor was because he thought it would solidify her place in his home with no escape.

He'd been right for too damn long.

"Hey, you alright?" Tara asked as she came out to the porch, her own cup of coffee clasped in her hands.

"I wasn't always like this," Callie said after a few minutes.

"Like what?" Tara asked.

"Nervous and scared, I guess. Weak," she whispered the last.

"You are not weak," Tara said fiercely, shaking her head. "You are so strong, Callie. You had to be to survive what you did and to take the chance you did that brought you here. That's not something someone weak would do. Nervous and scared, yeah, maybe, but that won't last forever."

"I hope you're right."

"I am," Tara said confidently. "I'm a really good judge of people as long as they aren't someone I'm sleeping with."

Callie laughed. "So which one of the handsome men I saw last night holds that honor?"

"None, unfortunately. I grew up with these guys and that's not to say I've never been with any of them, but it's never been serious and none of them are my forever."

"How can you be sure?"

Tara pressed her lips together and looked uncertain for a moment, not a look Callie had seen on the woman's face before. "Just a feeling I guess. I'm waiting for a spark that's undeniable. I want what Lance and Madeline have."

"That makes sense. I guess someday that's what I will be looking for too. But not for a long time. I can't imagine letting someone ..." Callie couldn't even finish the thought, she just shook her head and shivered. Imagining letting someone be intimate with her again was terrifying. Sex with Oliver hadn't been pleasurable since a year after they married and at times it had been downright painful.

Tara frowned at her with sympathetic eyes. "Don't let him rob you of a happy future, Callie. Take the time you need to heal—no one would think that's not okay— but don't let what he put you through take away any more of your happiness."

Callie nodded because she knew Tara was right. She didn't want that abusive asshole to take anything else away from her or Taylor ever again.

"I guess I need to take your advice, you moved past it. Even if you aren't dating anyone living here, you probably have someone stashed away in town." Callie sighed. "Someday I will too, but right now I just need to get me and Taylor somewhere safe and permanent."

"I hope you find what you're looking for," Tara said with a genuine smile.

"So, I understand you all grew up together, and you all moved here ..." Callie wasn't sure how to ask this woman if it was a cult.

"Kind of seems weird, huh?" Tara said with a laugh.

"Yeah, I mean, I first thought, motorcycle gang, but seems to be too many kids for that to be reasonable."

"Always lots of kids around," Tara agreed.

"Then I started to think of what else might keep people together. Is it a religious thing?"

Tara barked a laugh so loud everyone in the area turned to look. "You think we're a cult, don't you, oh my god, and Mick, he's our savior reborn, here to control us and get us through the pearly gates?" Tara laughed so hard she teared up and then Callie was laughing too because it was quite ridiculous. "Oh my god, oh my god," Tara panted. "I can just see Mick behind a pulpit glaring at us as he spouts out how we will go to hell if we don't follow his orders."

"Okay, so I figured that was a long shot, but still, what is keeping you all here together?"

Tara took some big breaths and settled herself. "Well, a lot of us lived together up north in Canada, fuck it was cold. We were pretty isolated in a little town and so we all took care of each other. I think that just bonded everyone. When some of us moved, most joined in going from place to place until we found this. Everyone seems to like it here." She shrugged as if it were simple, but Callie still had a feeling there was something more.

"As long as there are no sacrificial virgins or men with multiple wives," Callie said with a grin.

"Not at the moment, no," Tara said and Callie wasn't sure if she was being serious.

Taylor ran up then and shoved a frog in Callie's face. "Look what I caught!"

"Gross, but fun," Callie said pushing it away.

"You going to eat that?" Tara asked.

"What? No, super gross," Taylor said.

"Well then, leave nature alone if you aren't going to eat it, it was here before us," Tara said, chastising.

Taylor looked disappointed but turned to take the poor frog back where it had been captured from.

Over the next two weeks Callie stayed with Tara and worked at the clubhouse restaurant serving lunch and dinner nearly every day while Tara tended bar. She made friends with, or at least got to know the names of, everyone who lived in the old camp. Everyone was friendly and welcoming, no matter that most of the men were all tatted up and wore biker leathers half the time. They were never anything but respectful and nice to her. The women ranged from just as rough as the men to more soft like Madeline in her sundresses and curls, and all of them were sweet and welcoming too. Callie couldn't remember a time in her adult life where she'd had even one real friend and two weeks into this unexpected stay, she felt like she had one for sure and was well on her way to connecting with more.

The kids had continued to embrace Taylor as a new friend, and she couldn't imagine how hard it was going to be when they had to leave. She'd already torn him away from every friend he had back in Maine, not that he'd had many, Oliver didn't like Taylor going on playdates because it gave her the opportunity to interact with other mothers. This time would be even harder for both of them.

But before they could worry about that, her car remained the main issue. Lance told her the first part he ordered came in wrong, had to reorder, and the new one came in but didn't fix the issue so now he was waiting for another part. Meanwhile Mick ... Mick was an ever-present shadow lurking around her. She felt him everywhere and often at night stared out her bedroom window into the darkness and swore he was there. But she couldn't see anything in the darkness aside from the shadow of a dog, a very large dog that never seemed to be around during the daylight.

During the day Mick was always around but he avoided engaging her in conversation unless absolutely necessary. She was sure he resented that she'd stumbled into his life and now he was forced to pay her for work that could have been done by one of the other waitresses.

But the oddest part was how his lurking presence made her feel. It should have been disturbing, or creepy, but it wasn't. Every time she noticed he was near, she felt calm, safe, and cared for. As if he were her very own guard dog watching over her as she went about her day. It was a comfort she knew she'd miss when they left, and that realization made her all the more anxious to leave, she didn't want to depend on anyone. It wasn't safe.

MICK

The last two weeks had been increasingly torturous. His wolf was impatient to claim Callie, the animal didn't understand the need to go slow, to not scare her off. Mick understood it all too well. Callie had shared more and more with Tara about her time with her ex over the weeks and Tara had, of course, relayed it all to him. Every story made him crave the man's blood and realize that she was not going to welcome him into her life and bed any time soon.

Time was what they needed, but getting it wasn't easy. Lance kept giving Callie excuses about her car, but it wouldn't last forever and no matter how comfortable she and Taylor were getting with the pack, he knew she wasn't thinking it was permanent. She'd leave as soon as she could, but he knew he couldn't lose her, his wolf would go absolutely feral if he did.

Another thing that had begun to occur in the last two weeks was a connection built between him and the young boy, Taylor. After the first couple of days of getting comfortable with the group of pack children, Taylor had been bold enough to approach him outside the cabin one afternoon while his mother was working.

"You are pretty big, I bet you're really strong."

"I am ..." he said cautiously, unsure where this child's thoughts were going to lead.

"You take care of everyone. The other kids say you're in charge because you're the strongest."

Mick laughed. "Something like that, yes."

"You look at my mom with a frown a lot, but it's not like the way my dad frowned at her, it doesn't make my stomach hurt."

Mick had to swallow a growl in reaction to those words, the last thing he wanted was to frighten the boy. "My job is to protect everyone here, as long as you and your mom are here, I am going to keep you safe from everyone," he assured the boy.

"Yeah, that's what Sammy said but he also said that he has a tail so I'm not sure I can believe him," Taylor said with a shrug.

Mick darted his gaze over to where young Sammy was practically hiding behind a tree knowing he'd likely let out a secret his alpha wouldn't approve of.

"Well, wouldn't that be fun if your friend had a tail," Mick said, smiling at Taylor who agreed and ran off to rejoin the group of kids. He wondered if it wasn't best for Taylor to learn about what they were from his friends anyway, it would be less frightening than to see a full grown adult turn into a large wolf, something that was more and more likely to happen the longer they stayed here.

And the coming full moon was another problem because not only was the entire pack going to turn into wolves wanting to run and hunt, *his* wolf was going to be demanding he claim his unclaimed mate. The full moon's energy would give his wolf enough strength and control that there would be no reasoning with him, he'd overpower Mick and he would do whatever necessary to get to her, reveal himself to her and likely scare the fucking shit out of her in the process. Everything Mick had been desperate to avoid.

"I have to get her out of here," Mick growled to Lance from

behind his desk. The sound of hurrying feet through the clubhouse reminded Mick to keep his voice down.

"That's not your only option, you know that, right?" Lance countered. He'd been trying to get Mick to come clean to Callie the whole time, just put it all out there and see what she could handle.

"That's not an option," Mick snarled.

"So what are you going to do, want me to fix her car? Let her leave?"

"No!" Mick growled; he couldn't give her a means of escaping him.

"So then what?"

"I'm going to talk to Esmerelda and see if the witches will take them in for the night." There was a coven of witches in a nearby town, it was neutral territory and he knew she'd be safe there even without him to protect her.

Lance looked at Mick like he was insane. "How the hell are you going to convince her to go off and stay the night with strangers, you idiot?"

Mick threw his hands up in the air and cursed. "What the hell else am I supposed to do?"

"Fucking tell her!" Lance growled, his eyes yellow, showing that his wolf was close to the surface.

Mick felt his skin ripple, his own wolf just barely contained. He growled low and menacing and watched as Lance's wolf retreated, his eyes going back to brown and looking down in submission.

"I don't think I have a choice," Mick growled.

"No, I don't think you do either, but I think we disagree on what that choice is. Let me give you one other option. Let Madeline take her to the city for the night. She can tell Callie she wants to do some before baby shopping."

Mick shook his head. "Your mate shouldn't be away from you

on the full moon, especially pregnant. Lance, you know your wolf will go nuts."

"And what the fuck do you think yours is going to do when your mate is off with the witches, Mick? I love you, you're as much a brother to me as anyone could be and I respect you as my alpha, but this is the dumbest decision you've ever made."

Mick looked at his friend, desperate for answers and all he saw there was sympathy. That wasn't going to save Callie from his wolf's desires, and it wasn't going to save him when she inevitably ran away.

"Lock me up," Mick said.

"What? No, no way."

"It's the only viable option. You said it yourself. If I can't send her away, I need to be contained."

Lance shook his head in denial.

Before Mick could force him to promise he'd do it, the door burst open and Tara stood there looking angry enough to kill.

"What the fuck did you do now? Callie ran off crying, saying she was going to grab Taylor and find a way out of here because she heard *you* say you wanted to get her out of here?" Tara jabbed a finger in Mick's direction.

"That's not, ugh," Mick growled and sprinted from the office. How had he not realized she was so close? He'd been trying so hard lately to dampen his awareness of her, he hadn't sensed her lurking outside his office at all.

He opened himself back up to her and she was a beacon to his senses, he could smell her, and he could feel her. He followed her to Tara's cabin where she was throwing stuff in a bag. She was trembling and mumbling, and he hated that it was his fault again that she was upset. He wasn't cut out for this mate thing; he'd never been particularly good with emotions and females, and he'd never cared so much as he did now.

"What are you doing?" he demanded quietly.

She screamed and turned, holding a sweater against her chest like a shield, her eyes were wide, and she cowered slightly.

"Stop doing that," he snarled even though he knew it was the most ridiculous thing to ask of her.

"What? I'm sorry, I'm leaving okay, I know I've overstayed, I'll get a ride to town. I will get a hotel and when my car's done, I can pay Lance and—"

"Stop," he demanded and took a menacing step toward her. His wolf howling in fear, his eyes no doubt yellow with his wolf's need to burst out and claim this woman so she wouldn't leave him. "You aren't leaving."

Chapter 10

Callie

Callie wasn't sure what to think. She knew what she'd heard him say in his office. He wanted to get rid of her and she couldn't blame him. Obviously she was taking up space and money from the people he cared about here. She didn't belong, Taylor didn't belong, and they needed to move on. She had made enough money to stay a few nights in a hotel now so she was going to get out of his hair.

But why was he here looking like he wanted to shake her while demanding she stay?

Why was his glower and large presence in the tiny bedroom making her stomach tighten with something other than nerves?

She tried to keep her voice steady as she answered. "I heard you, you don't want us here, you're trying to find somewhere else for us to go," she whispered, a tremble in her voice despite her effort. "I'm sorry we overstayed, I'm sorry we stopped at all. I'm getting out of your way as fast as I can."

"You think I don't want you," he said, his voice almost a growl and a weird trick of the light made his eyes appear an eerie shade. He stepped closer to her and she gasped in a breath. Not sure if she was scared he was going to harm her, or hopeful that he was going to grab her, pull her against his hard body, and kiss her like she hadn't been kissed ever.

"I don't know what to think," she said honestly. She licked her lips and his gaze locked onto the motion. His obvious attention made her bite her lip. She heard a rumble come from him that was animalistic and raw. When his gaze met hers again his eyes were such a bright yellow she knew it couldn't be the light. "What?"

"Make no mistake, Callie. I want you. I want you and Taylor, and there's nothing that will take you two away from this pack. You are part of us now."

Before she could even process those strange words, he moved forward, erasing the distance between them. One large hand went to her lower back, pressing her body against his, his other went to the back of her head and pulled lightly on her hair to force her face up. Then his lips were on hers and all thoughts vanished from her mind. She melted against him. He was so warm and solid. She felt like he was surrounding her and keeping her together. His tongue begged entrance at her mouth, and she parted her lips for him. He swept in, tasting sweet, and filling her with an unfamiliar need. She clung to him, her hands fisting the shirt at his chest desperate to keep him close. She moaned as his tongue caressed hers. She felt as if she would die if she didn't have him right then. It was unlike anything she'd ever experienced before, and she wanted to follow it through to the promised incredible ending.

"Mom!" Taylor's voice from outside the cabin broke the spell and she pushed against Mick's chest. What was she thinking? She was a mother; she had no real job or home, and she was throwing herself at this man who may not even like her.

She was so confused.

Mick didn't let her go. His arms tightened on her and she looked up at him with fright, regret, and fear. Had she put herself into a situation where she would be harmed again?

"Fuck," he growled and let her go so suddenly she stumbled but his hand was quick to steady her as Taylor ran into the room.

"Look at this!" he yelled and shoved a large frog in her direction. "He keeps coming back to me, I think he likes me."

Callie used her years of trauma response and buried everything that had just occurred, steadied herself, and crouched to give Taylor her full attention. She praised his frog and instructed him to let it go free so it could be with its family.

"But, Mom ... I want to keep him, and I did let him go, he came back."

"No, that wouldn't be very nice to the frog. Sometimes what makes you happy is not what is best for someone else," she said, knowing she was saying it to herself too. Because jumping into bed with Mick would make her happy, but it could ruin Taylor's chance at happiness if she got herself into another situation where she was without options, without control, and living in fear. Mick's words ran through her head, *you are part of us now.* What did that mean? It felt so final, so consuming, and a part of her was terrified of it while another part wanted to embrace it and everything it might mean.

She just didn't know Mick well enough though, wasn't sure she'd ever be able to trust anyone even if she did know them for years. It was a depressing thought but all that mattered for the next eleven years was Taylor, his happiness, his ability to grow up and become a good person with a stable future.

When Taylor mumbled agreement and dragged his feet out of the cabin to do as she'd told him, Callie was surprised to see that Mick was gone too. She'd been so focused on Taylor, she hadn't noticed him leave.

Callie collapsed onto the bottom bunk and touched her lips. What did that kiss mean? Why was he so confusing, so hot and cold with her? She could only come up with one reasonable excuse, he was hiding something.

MICK

"She doesn't trust me," Mick snarled to Tara as he drank a whisky at the bar.

"Why should she? Sounds like you threw yourself at her then turned and ran like a fucking dickhead," Tara said it with a sweet smile.

"I left because she looked at me like I was about to force myself on her."

"You've spent two weeks ignoring her and then you practically attack her with your pent up desire, how's she supposed to figure out how she feels about you if you don't pick a direction? If I were her, I'd be hightailing it out of here, you're lucky she's basically stranded."

"She is my direction," he grumbled and slammed the rest of the whisky.

Tara leaned close and took the glass, "Lance told me what you asked him to do tomorrow."

Mick met his sister's eyes and saw pity there.

"I'll do it if he won't, and I'll figure out something to tell Callie."

"Thank you, Tara."

"But this is it. One moon is all you get. She needs to know before the next one, it isn't good for the pack to let this shit go on and it isn't good for *you*."

"I know," Mick said and walked out of the clubhouse. He wasn't convinced that there was any such thing as a good plan for the full moon, but he knew that he had to make his intentions clear before any other disasters could occur.

He made his way to her, following her scent. His wolf had latched onto it the first time he'd smelled her and would never be able to let it go. It drove his wolf crazy with the need to claim, mark and protect. Every day that he didn't do what his wolf wanted him to, his wolf got angrier, antsier, and that is why he needed to be safely away from Callie during the full moon. His wolf would be out, and he would not be able to resist her. That was not the way Mick wanted to reveal what he was to her, what they all were.

He was also terrified of setting the mate bond with her without knowing if he could really trust her with what it would mean, the power it would give her over him. Maybe more than anything else, that is what held him back and he wasn't sure how he'd ever trust her enough to give her that.

His wolf growled disagreement through his head.

Mick found Callie sitting on Tara's porch watching Taylor and the other young kids playing. She was in conversation with Jackson, a young single member of the pack. Old enough to be interested in a female and that made his wolf growl and claw at his insides. He lifted a lip and let out a low sound that had Jackson jumping up and scrambling away without even a goodbye.

Callie looked around confused, but when her eyes landed on him, they widened, and she stiffened.

Mick cursed himself for interrupting what had to be an innocent conversation, one in which she was obviously relaxed and unafraid. Now she looked like she wanted to run and hide.

Damnit how did he keep making her feel like that?

She was his mate and all he could manage to do was frighten her.

"Callie," he said before she could make a move to leave. He walked close but didn't sit down. "I—I want to take you out," he said.

"Oh ... um ..." she said and looked away, then down at her hands clutched in front of her, then back out toward Taylor. "I really can't, I mean Taylor ..."

"Tara will babysit, or Tiffany and Sarah love watching him, and I don't mean now. I mean night after next."

"Oh, my car isn't getting fixed any time soon, huh?"

"No," he said gruffly and she darted her gaze at him, eyes wide and he was cursing himself again. This was not going well. He closed his eyes, took a deep breath and made sure his voice was calm before he spoke again. "I am asking you out on a date, Callie. I want to date you." He wanted to claim her, fuck her and keep her forever. But a date would lead to the rest, it had to.

"A date? Mick, I don't think I'm ready for that," she answered with honesty and wrapped her arms around herself. "I don't know if I'll ever be," she whispered and looked out at Taylor. "I just need to take care of Taylor and figure out how I can best do that."

"Who's going to take care of you?" he asked and when she looked at him her eyes were filling with tears and her lip was trembling. "Let me take you out on a date, Callie. One date and I expect nothing from it but your undivided attention over a meal. You deserve to be cared for too, Callie, please."

Callie swallowed audibly and nodded.

That one small movement filled him with so much joy his wolf howled in his head, and he had to walk away before he was tempted to let the sound out of his own mouth.

CHAPTER 11

TARA

Tara watched Mick walk away from Callie with a cocky swagger and couldn't help smiling. She wouldn't tell Mick, but she'd worried the poor guy was never going to make progress with Callie. That he was destined to be forever wanting, knowing he'd had a mate, but she didn't choose him.

Her thoughts turned to Kody. That is the fate she was dooming him to. He didn't deserve to be punished for saving her. Allen had been going for another stab when Kody attacked. Allen would have finished the job and Tara would be dead right now if it wasn't for Kody.

She pulled out her phone and sent a text telling him she wanted to talk and to meet her at the territory boundary.

His response was immediate and enthusiastic, and it put a grin on her face.

She hurried to the spot that she'd started to think of as his. Across from a tree he spent so much time leaning against it smelled strongly of him even when he wasn't there. He was already waiting, breathing heavy as if he'd run as fast as he could, which was saying something for a shifter. When he spotted her, he straightened from the tree and stepped forward until he was toeing the invisible line that separated their territories. His eyes were wide and hopeful, but he didn't speak, just waited for her to either make all his dreams come true or crush his heart again.

Fuck, I really am a bitch.

"Hi," she said, not really sure how to start this conversation.

"Tara," he breathed the word, and the sound sent a tingle through her body.

"You've been very patient with me; I want you to know that I appreciate that."

"Tara, I would wait my entire life for you."

She took a deep breath and met his intense gaze. "I know that, and I don't want to make you wait any more."

His growl was deep and low, he took a tentative step over the line.

Tara stepped forward and she was wrapped in his long hard arms, he tucked her head against his chest and just held her. "My mate," he whispered and kissed the top of her head. "Come to my den."

Tara pulled back and he let her go without hesitation but there was a pain in his eyes. "No. You know that isn't safe. Kyr would use it as an excuse to start a war if I was in your territory."

"You are my mate. I will tell the elders; I will claim you officially and Kyr won't be able to say a damn thing about it."

Tara smiled and reached out to touch his face. He was so unafraid, so willing to put it all out there and she loved that, it thrilled her even as it terrified her. "I don't think I'm ready for all that. Can we take it slow? We can get together after the full moon and talk things through. We're going farther tomorrow than usual because of the humans in our territory so I need to go make some preparations now. When I'm back, we will figure it all out."

She pushed forward and kissed him quickly then turned and ran before she could be tempted to do more. She couldn't hide the huge smile on her face, or the scent of bear that clung to her, and she didn't want to. She wanted to bathe in his scent so everyone would know who she belonged to.

She ran by Simone out on patrol. The wolf paused and sniffed in her direction then gave her an approving nod. No one here was going to judge her. She hoped Kody's clan felt the same when he revealed it to them.

Kody

Kody watched her go, his heart beating wildly. She was finally accepting him. It was a small step, but it was a step, and he wanted to shout about it to the sky. But he couldn't, not yet. He needed to confront Kyr.

He stalked back to the center of their territory and straight to Kyr's den. He didn't bother knocking on the screen, just pushed inside and growled at the woman sitting next to Kyr with her shirt around her waist and skirt hiked up.

"What the fuck!" Kyr snarled.

"Get out, Ava," Kody growled. "And you'd better tell your dad what you were doing here, or I will."

Ava didn't hesitate, she jumped up and fixed her clothes as she ran from the room with a look of terror on her face.

When the screen banged shut behind her Kyr grabbed a beer off the cluttered coffee table and glared at his brother.

"What the fuck is wrong with you, Kyr? She's only nineteen."

"She's old enough, and do you see a lot of other options around here? That little female from the south isn't going to give me strong cubs and Patrice is too old to give me as many as I deserve."

"You have a possible mate coming from Alaska," Kody growled.

"She cancelled," Kyr grunted.

Kody was taken off guard, although Kyr had kept it from him, it had apparently been arranged for months. The Alaska clan was low on members too, looking for ways to expand and had seemed happy to send a possible mate down to an alpha. "Why?"

"Her father called it off, said he didn't trust this pack to take proper care of his daughter," Kyr snarled.

Kody knew his brother wanted to blame him, wanted to say it was about the wolf packs so close and unchallenged, but Kody had a feeling it had everything to do with the way Kyr and some of the others treated the few females that were here. Someone must have tipped them off, probably the clan member that had been sent down to inspect them last week. Kody wanted to punch his brother. He wanted to throttle him, and not for the first time. He wanted to force Kyr to step down as leader of this clan because he was doing a shit job of it.

But he didn't. Kody had walked into Kyr's trailer ready to calmly lay out the facts of what was going to happen with Tara and he couldn't do that if he got in a fight with Kyr about the way he ran things. So he gritted his teeth and took a breath.

"When the pack gets back from their full moon trip I'm taking Tara on a date. She's agreed to see what this mate thing between us could be."

Kyr's eyes flared with anger. "You are a disgrace, Kody, you know that? A fucking disgrace, do you have any idea what Dad would say if he knew you were trying to mate with a wolf?"

Kody stood stiff, his chin notched up, he didn't dare point out that their dad would kick Kyr's ass for messing with a barely legal clan member. It was the clan alpha's job to protect the clan, not to take advantage of his position.

Kody bared his teeth at Kyr but his brother seemed unbothered, just drank his beer and shook his head.

"That little southern bear, Laura, she likes you, why not just take what she's got? She barely speaks to anyone else. I tell you what, you fuck that wolf bitch, get it out of your system, then claim Laura and get it over with, our clan needs members. I'm breeding Ava, maybe Patrice too, I'm doing my duty." He stood then and poked Kody in the chest. "You are going to do your fucking duty, too."

Kody reacted like he'd never done before, always so careful to show his minutes-older brother respect, to not get into it with him because he was afraid to lose, and he was afraid to win. He didn't want to lead this clan; he just wanted to live his life and keep his promise to their father that he'd always support Kyr. But he couldn't let Kyr get away with this shit he was spouting. He grabbed his brother around his thick neck and snarled in his face. "Tara is my *mate*, and I will breed her, no other," he spat and walked out of the trailer.

His phone buzzed as he stalked toward the woods, and he answered without looking.

"Hey there, big guy. I'm ready to call in our date."

Kody froze, Janet's sultry voice making his stomach turn. "I can't."

She just laughed. "Oh, you will, or else I will be telling Tara what you did. Dinner, night after the full moon. You know the moon makes me horny." She hung up without waiting for his answer.

CHAPTER 12

CALLIE

Callie couldn't believe she'd actually agreed to go on a date with that terrifying man. As she washed tables the next afternoon in the clubhouse she couldn't stop playing his words over and over in her head. *Who's going to take care of you? You deserve to be cared for, too.* No one had cared for her in so long and she craved it. Almost as much as she craved the feel of his lips against hers again.

"I'm in trouble," she mumbled. He may be taking her on a date with nothing else in mind, but could her heart and body resist any advances he decided to try out?

She seriously doubted it.

"So I hear you're planning a date with my big brother," Tara said as she waltzed into the room.

"I—uh, yeah is that okay? Is that weird for you?" She'd hate to have anything ruin the friendship she'd developed with Tara, even if she didn't plan to stay here longer than necessary, she hoped to keep some kind of friend connection with the woman who had helped her so much.

"Weird? Are you kidding me, I think it's amazing, his grumpy ass needs a girlfriend."

"That's a strong word," Callie grumbled.

"Grumpy ass? Sorry, I know you don't like cussing, but the kids aren't around."

Callie rolled her eyes at Tara's intentional misunderstanding. "No, girlfriend. It's just one casual date, nothing more."

"Sure, whatever you have to tell yourself," Tara said with a grin that had Callie's cheeks heating. "By the way, no need to open for dinner. We can close up now that the lunch rush is done."

"Why?"

"Everyone who isn't under fifteen or pregnant is going camping remember, I told you last night, though you were a little distracted," she laughed. "I assume you don't want to go sleep on the ground around a fire? Though Mick would probably be happy to share his sleeping bag," she said with an exaggerated eye roll.

"Oh, yeah no I'm not a big camping girl, yeah I remember you saying something about it," she didn't, last night she had been replaying Mick's kiss and Mick's words over and over in her head and noticed nothing else. "And I wouldn't want to leave Taylor overnight."

"Great, you're on babysitting duty then. The kids mostly care for themselves, the super young ones stay with the preggos like Madeline. So you'll just be available in case someone breaks a leg."

"Great, because I don't have a working car and I don't know where the hospital is," she said with a heavy sigh.

"That was a joke, mostly. So anyway, you can head out, we'll open again for dinner tomorrow, you'll be with Mick though so no worries about that. You get a whole day off!"

More like many, *many* worries, Callie wanted to say but didn't. What did Mick expect, did he think one date meant they were *dating?* Should she talk to him, should she talk to Taylor? What was he going to think about all this and fuck, technically she was still married so she probably shouldn't even go on one date ... but she wanted to, she really wanted to. It didn't have to be serious, and she wouldn't make a big deal about it to Taylor, just friends eating a meal. Nothing wrong with that.

Somehow she doubted that Mick felt it was that casual and the thought warmed and excited her.

A couple hours later Callie was enjoying the extra moments of free time and deciding rather quickly that she didn't want free time. She'd become very dependent on working to keep her mind occupied and off of the future, off of the past, and a little bit off of the now.

Her gaze tracked Mick as he walked through the clearing. Kids surrounded him shouting and talking and practically glowing under his attention. How could a man who looked like he would rather punch someone in the face than have a conversation with them be so obviously adored by children and adults.

She didn't understand what this place was really all about and the fact that everyone was apparently going on a big sleep out in the woods together tonight didn't clarify anything more for her. But the joy she saw in the children told her one very important thing. Whatever this was, it was good, and it was safe.

Mick noticed her watching and said something that had the kids scattering with giggles as he made his way to her.

"You talked to Tara?" he asked.

"About tonight? Yeah," she said. "I am in charge if anyone breaks a leg," she tried to sound light and joking.

He nodded and rubbed the back of his neck. "Okay, well, it's getting about time to leave so I'll see you tomorrow, stay safe, okay."

"You too, there's a lot of wolves out there, I hear the damn things all night long. I know Tara says they don't bother people but still, if you get in their territory I'm sure they'll react."

Mick grunted a laugh. "Don't worry about me, I know how to handle a wolf."

Callie frowned, not liking the idea of him killing any animal just because he'd happened to wander too close, but she kept the thought to herself.

Mick leaned down and touched her chin, forcing her head up until she met his gaze. "I am really looking forward to tomorrow night, Callie."

Her cheeks reddened and a warmth swirled in her belly as she watched his eyes narrow with an intense yellow glint in them that she'd seen before. It had to be a trick of the light, no one's eyes changed like that. He closed the distance between them and pressed his lips to hers. One quick soft kiss then he was straightening and walking away toward the clubhouse.

Callie turned from watching his back retreat and saw that a few of the kids were watching her and giggling. Taylor was among them, staring at her with a look on his face she didn't understand. It wasn't anger, it wasn't mirth like the other children at seeing adults kiss, it was something else. Callie stood, ready to gather him in her arms and ask him what he was thinking, to reassure him and tell him that she'll cancel the date with Mick if it made him uncomfortable.

What was she thinking? She couldn't date someone. She couldn't kiss someone. Taylor was the only important thing in her life, and she'd do anything, *was* doing anything she could, to make sure he was safe and happy. Her heart tore as he stared at her then turned and joined back in the game he'd been playing with the kids.

Callie sat back down and bit her nails. She'd ask him about it later. Shit, she would cancel on Mick if Taylor was uncomfortable but a part of her would be sad to do it.

With so many gone camping the place was quiet in comparison to the normal chatter of so many friends living so close together. Three women were pregnant and at their homes with a troop of young kids to watch over. There was a large group of older kids that were still too young to go camping apparently, who were gathered in the clearing playing games and with Taylor among them Callie was happy to keep an eye. The sun had set and there didn't seem to be any end in sight for the youngsters and their games.

"Can we roast marshmallows and hot dogs?" Taylor ran up to her to ask.

"I don't see why not. I bet I can find some at the clubhouse. I'll go look." She didn't think Mick would mind her taking a few supplies to feed the kids and if he did, well, she'd pay him back.

"Thanks, Mom," Taylor yelled as he ran back to the group to announce his mom was getting them food.

Callie walked to the clubhouse which was unusually dark for this time of evening. Typically it was full of rowdy people until the early hours. After the dinner rush and most of the families left it was more bar and club than diner; but it stayed safe. Callie supposed it was because they all lived here, if anyone got out of hand they'd have to deal with the embarrassment every day after when they looked at their friends.

This place had become a safe haven for her and Taylor and she knew she'd be sad to leave it when they did. But would she be safe staying? She didn't know. Didn't know if Oliver was after her. He had to be, right? He had told her multiple times that she could never get away from him and she believed that. Even now she believed if she didn't keep running he'd catch up and she'd be dead or worse, because there were definitely things worse than death and she'd seen them in Oliver's eyes many times.

Having Mick and everyone else around made her feel like there was a wall between her and the possibility of Oliver. But tonight that wall was gone, and she was feeling the fear and urgency that was never far, creep back on her.

She stopped outside the door, her eye caught on a clump of hair, it was a dark brown color and when she picked it up it felt coarse in her hand. She wasn't an animal expert but she didn't think this was from a dog or even a wolf like she suspected were close. A new fear spiked through her, could it be a bear? Tara had assured her that no bears had ever come into the camp area but she'd also told Callie that if she ever saw one to stay well clear of it and tell someone right away.

She decided she'd keep the clump and ask one of the other adults about it just in case it meant a bear had been sniffing around their dumpsters, something she felt was very likely.

She rushed into the dark building, in a hurry to get back to the kids and warn them about the possibility of bears, maybe send them all to their homes sooner rather than later. She searched the kitchen first. No luck there. Then stood in the middle of the kitchen and looked at the door she'd never been through before. It led to the basement where food was stored, extra beer, and supplies. She'd never been the one to go down and fetch it, there had always been someone else eager to make the trek for her when necessary and she'd appreciated that, not anxious to walk down into a dark basement with a door at the top that locked. But she knew where the key was, it was right there hanging next to it as if they weren't really trying to keep people out of it, they were prepared to keep something in.

Callie shook her head and chastised herself, that was ridiculous. She was being ridiculous and no one else was here so she was perfectly safe. She notched up her chin and walked to the door, it was locked, which was odd because she'd never seen anyone who needed to go down there have to unlock the door. But maybe because they weren't open tonight, they'd locked it up? It would make sense too with most of the cabins empty because of the camping trip, it was reasonable to lock up valuables.

Hands a bit shaky, she pulled the key off the hook and unlocked the door. The click was loud in the silence of the empty kitchen and her heart skipped a beat as she waited for something to happen.

Of course nothing did and she chastised herself again for being such a scaredy cat. She opened the door and the whoosh of air held a scent that had the hair on the back of her neck standing up. Not a sound reached her though and she felt around for the light switch. She flipped it and it illuminated the stairwell. She could see a few shelves near the bottom stacked with restaurant supplies. It looked perfectly safe and exactly as she'd expect restaurant storage to be.

"I'm an idiot," she grumbled and forced herself to walk down. She reached the bottom and started searching the shelves for what she needed. Two bags of marshmallows and a pack of buns were easy to find, but she needed more hot dogs so she walked around a packed shelf hoping to find the extra refrigerator.

And froze.

There was a huge cage with an enormous black wolf locked inside. Its wide yellow eyes were locked on her as it stood there, pressed against the bars as if it were trying to get as close to her as possible.

She gasped and the wolf growled. She stepped back, running into a rack of beer and it pushed against the bars.

She turned to run and heard the bars shake as the wolf threw its enormous body against the cage.

Would it hold? Was this why no one let her down here?

She slipped on the stairs as she scrambled and hit her knee, crying out in pain and panic. Blood seeped from the wound, but it barely slowed her down as the sounds of the wolf trying to escape increased. As soon as she got through the door at the top she slammed it behind her only to realize she'd dropped the key downstairs somewhere. No time to go back for it by the sound of loud crashing that had to be the wolf escaping and knocking over racks of food and beer.

Callie bolted for the front of the clubhouse. She couldn't lead the thing back to the children. If she could make it to her car she could get her gun, she could protect herself and the kids.

As she reached the front door of the clubhouse she heard the splintering of the basement door. She flew across the porch and down the front steps then raced to her car, yanking the passenger door open, she grabbed the gun from the glovebox and turned just in time to see the black wolf jump at her from the porch.

She didn't think, she just shot.

MICK

Mick went down, the shot wasn't fatal, but it was enough to give him pause and bring his mind forward through the haze of the wolf. Callie was in danger, but it wasn't from him or the wolf. His wolf had caught the scent of a dangerous predator when she was standing in front of his cage. He could have held his wolf back from her if he hadn't scented it, but his wolf would never let her be threatened.

He hadn't expected this reaction from her, she was amazing. Standing there with the gun still raised, a surprised and frightened look on her face but also a determination in her stance. She was protecting herself and the kids. That had to be why she ran this way and not back toward the safety of the cabins and possible help. She was leading what she thought was the danger, away from the kids.

But she'd put herself closer to the real danger in the process without realizing it. A danger his wolf was anxious to attack but he held it steady. If he stood up now, he knew she'd likely shoot at him again. The first bullet had hit his hind leg and it hurt, but he could easily ignore it and he wasn't about to die.

Steady. He told his wolf. *We can't protect her if she shoots us too many times.*

His wolf growled disagreement. It wanted to rush out and herd her to safety, search out where she was wounded—he could smell her blood—and find the bear that he could smell on her.

And then mark her as his.

She was moving slowly, putting the car between them but her eyes weren't leaving him. She smelled like terror, and he hated that it was directed at him. This is exactly what he'd been trying to avoid by having Tara lock him up down there.

A deep growl behind Callie had her turning and that was when he moved. He jumped up to the top of her car then leaped over her, landing between her and the bear shifter that was standing at the edge of the woods now, lip curled back in a snarl.

He just hoped Callie wouldn't shoot him again. Would she realize he wasn't the threat? He raised the hair on his back and growled at the bear, warning him to back off. Why the hell was he here in Mick's territory?

The bear slammed his front paws back down on the ground and growled a challenge.

Mick met it, racing forward to keep the bear from getting any closer to Callie. He'd wrestled a bear before, slightly smaller and neither really trying to kill the other, but this was different. This was Kyr and he wanted blood.

Mick would die to protect his mate and pack, but he hoped he didn't have to.

The fight was vicious, sharp pains penetrated him as he fought. Mick knew he'd be broken and bleeding by the end even if he did win.

A howl in the distance told him that his pack had caught what was going on. They could feel what he was feeling but they were too far away to help, he couldn't wait for them, he had to fight with all he had.

Kyr knocked him back, Mick landed belly up and Kyr roared

as he stood on hind legs, ready to pounce on him. Mick rolled to escape and jumped up. Kyr was facing Callie now, ready to go after her. Mick slammed into Kyr's side, taking a bite out of his thick flesh and drawing Kyr's attention back to him.

Kyr swiped at Mick and caught his head, knocking him to the side and rattling his brain for a moment. As Mick focused back, he heard two shots ring out and waited for the sting of bullets.

They didn't come. He jumped to his feet and turned back to the bear. Kyr was lying motionless on the ground, a bleeding hole where his eye had been.

Mick turned to Callie who stood gasping and shaking by the car, gun barely hanging in her limp hand. He took one step toward her and she lifted the gun, shooting him in the shoulder.

That was the last thing he could take. Exhausted and bleeding, knowing his mate wasn't about to be eaten by a bear, he collapsed.

CHAPTER 13

CALLIE

Callie stood frozen in place, chest heaving as she waited for another attack. Whatever horrible beast might be coming at her next. When the world around her remained quiet aside from the shouts of the older children, no doubt running in her direction because of the gunshots, she relaxed, ready to tell them to stay away from this gruesome scene. She turned back to the dead animals and the gun dropped from her trembling hands as she watched the two morph into naked and bleeding men. A horrified scream burst from her throat and she poised to run but then her gaze locked on the wolf who was now a man covered in tattoos. Her eyes swept up his arms and to his neck where the tattoos continued, she knew they would peek out of his shirt there. And now she knew they covered nearly every inch of skin from his neck to his waist and a few on his legs as well.

Her disbelief and horror turned to concern. "Mick," she whispered and ran to him.

He was bleeding from wounds all over his body and she pressed her fingers to his neck, feeling for a pulse.

"What happened?" Madeline asked as she waddled up with a string of the older kids in tow.

"I—I didn't know it was Mick," Callie wailed.

Madeline touched her shoulder and knelt, her voice calm. "Of course not, and that's his fault. Let me see," she said and reached out, pushing Callie's hands away from the bloody neck and pressed her own fingers there. "He's alive. The pack's coming. We need to move him inside and see what we're dealing with."

Callie sat back, thankful someone else was there to take charge. The other pregnant women were coming too, she noticed. Bridgette and Flora, both far less pregnant than Madeline, were hurrying to the scene with looks of concern but no blame. They started ordering the older kids to go back and watch the younger kids at the cabins and grabbed a couple of the oldest boys to lift Mick and carry him into the clubhouse.

Callie was impressed by the strength of the two young teens as they hefted the large man and took him away.

Madeline put a hand on her back and stared into her eyes. "Callie, do you understand?"

Callie shook her head no.

"Okay, that's fine, but I need you to go with Mick. Stay with him, okay? Your presence is going to help him get better. If he wakes up and you're not there, he's going to freak out and try to move, we need him to stay still so his wounds can be sewed up."

Callie didn't understand but she let Madeline and Flora help her stand and walked her into the clubhouse where the boys had laid Mick on one of the larger tables. They were already working on cleaning the blood and dirt off of him.

Bridgette walked out of the office with a large first aid kit and a determined look on her face. She ordered the boys and Flora to hold Mick down and then, Callie could only watch with horror as the woman removed a bullet that she knew she'd put there. Mick didn't move at first but by the time Bridgette was working on the second bullet hole he jerked, and his eyes flew open. They were fully yellow, and he growled, swinging out at Bridgette.

Madeline pushed Callie closer to him and she couldn't hold

back a scream, he was going to hit *her*, he was going to be so pissed, she'd shot him twice! Mick's eyes latched on to her and he growled a different deeper sound then reached out and grabbed her arm in a bruising grip before falling back, passed-out once more.

"Fuck, work fast, Bridgette," Madeline said.

"I didn't know. I didn't mean to," Callie stammered as Bridgette closed the hole on his leg.

"This is why we all told him he had to tell you before tonight," Flora said. "Drink this." She handed Callie a glass with amber liquid and she didn't even care what it was, she shot back the drink and coughed as it burned her throat.

"Pack's here," Madeline said. "I'll go out there and let them know the situation, stay here," she told Callie firmly. "Don't leave his side no matter what." Then Madeline left the clubhouse.

"Pack," Callie murmured trying to piece everything together but she couldn't, it didn't make sense. Nothing made sense. Not even what she had witnessed or done.

A few minutes later Tara and Lance rushed in looking like they were just pulling on their clothes. Lance and Tara rushed in, Lance to Mick and Tara to Callie.

"Oh my god, are you okay? What the hell happened?" Her eyes swept down her body. "You're bleeding."

Callie blinked and tried to corral her thoughts into order as she looked at Tara whose eyes were glowing an eerie yellow. "The kids wanted marshmallows and hot dogs," she finally managed.

"Shit, did you go downstairs? Did Mick attack you?"

"He," she stopped and looked down at the bleeding man. She wasn't sure what to say, didn't understand what had happened. "A wolf chased me up the stairs. There was a bear outside."

Tara pulled her in for a tight hug. "Saw that. Kyr."

"Is it ... did I ..." Callie couldn't finish the sentence. Had she killed a man?

"You protected yourself and the kids." Tara said, her voice soft and soothing. She pet Callie's hair and kept her gaze. "You acted in self defense. You and everyone who was still here was in danger from Kyr."

Callie nodded but tears streamed down her face. She'd killed someone.

"Do you want me to take you back to the cabin so you can lie down? Does your knee need stitches?"

Callie didn't know what she needed or wanted, she stared down at Mick, afraid she would be responsible for his death too. Her knee didn't even hurt anymore so she was sure she didn't need stitches. "I'm okay, Madeline said I should stay. How can I help? Should we take him to the hospital?"

"Bridgette is a nurse, he'll be okay. He is going to heal fast alright, don't worry, but you being near will be good for him, especially if he wakes up before she's done."

Callie didn't understand why her presence would help him, but she wanted to be sure he was going to live so she stepped closer.

"Hold his hand, Callie, this one's going to hurt," Bridgette said as she prodded around a large gash in his side.

Callie grabbed his hand in both of hers and brought it to her chest, she stared at his face, not able to stomach the wounds on his body and prayed to whatever goddess might be listening that this man wake up when this was over and not kill her for shooting him, twice.

Someone pushed a chair behind her knees and she sat. She continued to clutch Mick's hand like it was the only thing keeping him alive. Bridgette finished suturing wounds and Callie finally had to let Mick's hand go so Lance could lift him and carry him to his cabin. She followed close, arms wrapped tightly around herself. When they exited the clubhouse out the back, she noticed the entire community standing around with pained looks.

Callie froze, knowing this was all her fault, she'd done this, wouldn't they hate her? Tara put an arm around her and pushed her forward. Some of the people standing around did look at her but it was with wariness more than blame or anger.

"Mom, what happened?" Taylor asked, running up to her.

She reached down and caught him mid leap, pulling him into her arms easily as she walked. She squeezed him tight, and he wrapped his little body around her, squeezing back just as tight.

"Are you alright? We heard shots and I wanted to come make sure you were okay, but the bigger kids wouldn't let me! And then everyone was here, and they were talking about Mick. They said you were okay but—but Mom," his voice dropped to a barely audible whisper. "You're bleeding, did he hurt you? Do we have to leave?"

Callie's heart broke for the worry in her son's tone and although they didn't have to leave because Mick had done anything wrong, they did need to leave eventually. This wasn't the place for them, she thought now more than ever that had to be true.

"We're staying until the car is fixed, you know that," she said back.

"But did he hurt you, Mom, like Dad used to?"

All around her it seemed not another noise was heard even as they continued to walk, and the entire community surrounded them like a silent protective detail. She knew they were all hearing this hushed conversation. "Mick didn't hurt me, baby, there was just a bear," she said, and she swore she heard breaths of relief throughout the group. Were they worried Mick would hurt her?

"I thought the wolves kept the bears away, that's what Peter told me," Taylor said, his young brain switching quickly out of his worry for his mother's safety. "Wolves are way stronger and scarier than bears."

"I don't know," she admitted because it was a subject she really didn't want to talk about, especially not with Taylor.

"How about I take Taylor back to the cabin and put him to

bed," Tara said when they reached Mick's cabin. "You stay here with Mick; he'll want to see you when he wakes up."

"Oh I don't think—" she began but Tara just wrestled Taylor onto her back and rolled her eyes at Callie.

"Yeah, he will. Stay here Callie."

Callie watched Tara walk away with Taylor laughing on her back as she bumped and ran then turned to the door of Mick's cabin. Bridgette was holding it open for her. She walked in feeling like she was invading his privacy. He'd never invited her to his place, and it felt somehow way too personal to be in it. It was clean; she was surprised for a bachelor. Set up just like Tara's, it had a small living room and kitchen, loft upstairs and bedroom downstairs. All of it was decorated in grey and black, which didn't surprise her at all, those seemed to be the only colors he ever wore too. But despite its very masculine look, it felt comfortable.

She walked up to the loft and her anxiety amped up again, she was entering his bedroom, this had to be violating his trust in some way. Lance smiled at her as she entered, he had laid Mick on the bed and covered him in a blanket which she was thankful for. Now that he wasn't bleeding it was hard not to take a look at his body. And she definitely did. It was covered in tattoos she wanted to explore and all muscular and tan like he must spend time naked in the sun. Not to mention a very large part of him had made her immediately blush, catch her breath, and avert her gaze. She'd only ever seen Oliver's and it did *not* look anywhere near as impressive. In fact she'd always been a bit repulsed by Oliver's pale and pink limpish thing. But Mick's ... well it made her think of things she'd only ever read in books in the library because she didn't dare let Oliver know what she was reading.

"Sit and sleep next to him. You won't hurt him, he's already healing," Bridgette said from behind her.

"Oh no, I don't think I could sleep in here."

Bridgette just shrugged. "Suit yourself, I need to go home and sleep." She rubbed her little baby bump and turned. "Oh, make sure he eats and drinks water when he wakes up," she called over her shoulder.

Callie looked at Lance who was still standing by Mick. He didn't move or speak, just stared down at his passed-out friend until the front door closed behind Bridgette.

"If you are going to leave it's better to do it before he wakes up. I'll have your car running in five minutes." He paused as the meaning behind that bit of information swirled through her and lifted his gaze to meet hers. "But know that if you do leave, he's as good as dead because his wolf has chosen you. The moment you walked into the clubhouse it was over for him. He'd never hurt you, never force you to be here or be with him, but if you leave, it will destroy him. I'm his second in command and if he goes feral because you're gone, it's my responsibility to put him down."

Callie didn't know what to say to that, so she just walked close to the bed and kneeled by Mick's head. "He's not going to hurt me?"

"He could never."

"Then why was he chasing me, why was he locked in a cage?"

"That's his story to tell, Callie, and I'm sure he will when he wakes up. If you don't think you can handle the answers, don't be here when he does."

With those dooming words Lance walked out of the room and out of the cabin.

Callie didn't know what to do, but she knew she couldn't leave, not without knowing what all this was about. She pulled his hand out from under the cover and gripped it between hers again, then laid her head on the bed and soon fell asleep.

CHAPTER 14

TARA

Tara rushed back to the dead body as soon as Taylor was asleep. Most of the pack had shifted back to wolf form because of the full moon's call and she itched to do the same, but the joy of it wasn't there. Usually they shifted and ran and chased and enjoyed the night of celebration, but it was tainted with Mick hurt and the question of what the death of Kyr was going to mean.

She pulled out her cellphone and called Kody, he needed to know what had happened. If the bears were linked in the same way that the wolves were, he'd have felt the death, the whole clan would have and if they knew Kyr had come up here, they could be ready to attack at any moment.

"Tara, I can't talk right now—"

"Kyr is here, shot dead by Mick's mate," she hurried to explain before he could finish.

Silence met her words.

"Kody?"

"I'm here."

"He attacked, why the hell was he up here anyway?" Tara demanded.

"I don't know, Tara. I'm coming for the body."

"It's out front of the clubhouse. Please hurry," she begged as she looked at the bleeding naked body of a man who had caused so much trouble since they'd moved here.

"I'm coming as fast as I can, is it safe for me to come through pack land?"

"I'll meet you at the border," she said and hung up then shifted, tearing up her clothes as she did, running as fast as she could to meet him.

Lance moved in beside her and Brad on her other flank. Together the three of them skidded to a halt at the border where two bears paced back and forth, neither was Kody.

Lance and Brad growled, the bears roared, and Tara shifted back to human. "I'm meeting Kody, taking him to the body," she said.

They answered with roars and more pacing.

"He came into our territory, attacked a human and she shot him," Tara snarled. "This is not an invitation to start a war that will only hurt both sides."

"She's right, get out of here, both of you. Gather the clan, we've got an alpha to burn," Kody said as he strode up. His eyes were locked onto Tara even as he ordered the others around. A fire lit in them as he took in her nakedness.

"Follow me," she said and shifted again, not able to stand there naked and human with him looking like he wanted to devour her. She yipped and the three wolves turned, they started to run, Kody close behind. As they moved farther into the territory more wolves joined the procession, some on two legs, some four. No one spoke and there was a feeling of contempt that rolled through the pack. Tara tried to project calm, to project peace, but she wasn't alpha, she wasn't even very dominant and as second, Lance was in charge now until Mick woke up.

Tara caught Lance's eye and he nodded understanding, no one would attack Kody, but that didn't mean they had to like that he was here.

Kody didn't speak, just picked up his brother and turned. He walked back to the border silently, the wolves following. When he was once again in bear clan territory, he turned to face them all. His eyes were on Tara, but his words were for the whole pack.

"I am alpha of this bear clan now; I have no issue with your pack."

He turned then and walked on, bears falling in behind him as he went.

Her pack dispersed but Tara sat there and stared, long after the last bear disappeared. What did it mean that Kody was the alpha now?

KODY

Kody carried Kyr's body to a clearing behind the trailers. The clan was already gathered there, as tradition dictated, they would burn the body and they would shift, staying in bear form until the last ember was cold.

He set his brother on the carefully laid pile of wood. The elders moved forward, all to touch Kyr and bless his journey to the afterlife. After the last blessing had been said Kody turned to face the clan, he was handed the torch that would light his brother's pyre and he took a deep breath, meeting each member's eyes briefly, making certain they were with him, that there would be no challenge to his role as alpha. When he got to Ava he flinched at the black eye the young woman had, no doubt from her father. Either because she'd been with Kyr or because she hadn't been smart enough to get a proposal beforehand, perhaps simply because she'd been caught.

As he looked into her eyes he saw a spark of hope there that had him quickly moving on, he had no interest in her, even if he wasn't meant for Tara he wouldn't want someone so young and inexperienced.

"My brother went into the pack's territory and attacked a

human. The human shot him. There will be no repercussions against the wolf pack or the human among them," he stated firmly and glowered at any who made noise of disagreement.

When everyone was looking down and silent, he lit up the pyre and said one final *fuck you* to his brother. Kyr wasn't a great man, or a good leader, and the clan was better off without him.

One big obstacle to his happiness with his mate was gone and he could only be thankful, but another one loomed farther to the north.

He had to deal with Janet.

CHAPTER 15

MICK

Mick smelled her; citrus and sunshine surrounded him. He thought it had to be a dream, a dream he didn't want to wake up from, so he kept still and his eyes closed, afraid if he woke up completely she'd be gone. Not just gone from his side either, but gone from the camp, gone from his life forever, and he knew he wouldn't survive that.

A small noise had him opening his eyes and he was relieved to see that she was there, filling his home with her sweet scent, a scent he could never in a million lifetimes forget. She had his hand gripped between hers and her head resting on his bed as she slept, mouth open and drooling just a little in the most delightfully endearing way. He thought he could watch her sleep forever but then her forehead scrunched, her body tensed, and she made a noise again, a small, pained, noise as if she were having a nightmare.

That was something he wouldn't stand for, no one harmed her, not even in her own damn dreams.

He lifted his other hand and that's when he felt every ache and pain in his body from the attack. He groaned as he moved to stroke her hair softly and wake her up, but the sound he made was more than enough. She flew awake, scrambling away from the bed and staring at him with wide, fearful eyes.

"Callie," he grunted, letting his arm drop. This is what he'd been worried about, she feared him now, saw him as a monster.

"Mick, I'm sorry, I shouldn't be here. I know I'm the last person you want to see."

He grunted a laugh and it hurt, which made him groan and then she backed away farther, pressing herself against the loft railing.

"I'll go get Tara or Bridgette," she said and turned, fleeing down the stairs and out the front door before he could stop her.

A few minutes later Tara strolled in, looking pissy. "What the fuck, it's not her fault she shot you, you were a scary wolf."

"I didn't say I blamed her—I didn't fucking say anything—she just ran away like a spooked deer."

"Well you're lucky she's not leaving, yet. Lance fixed her car last night. I told her you deserved to hear an apology from her, not me, but I told her I'd come check on you first, make sure you weren't out for blood."

"It's definitely not her *blood* I want."

"Even though she shot you twice?" Tara asked with a wink.

Mick growled at his sister and sat up with a groan, that bear had really gotten him good. "She also shot that bear shifter twice. I need to talk to Lance, has anyone heard from the bear clan?"

"Want my advice?" she asked instead of answering his question.

"No," he growled and swung his feet over the side of the bed.

"Well, you get it anyway. You need to lay your ass back in that bed, you need to play this for everything and let her care for you. Let her see you weak, let her apologize through actions while you show her that you aren't angry. Most of all, let her see that you're a safe place and she can trust you even after the absolute worst she can do."

"The worst she could do is leave," he grumbled but laid back down because he saw the wisdom in Tara's words.

"Great, I'll tell her you are in need of care and would love to see her and you aren't mad but want to explain everything. Which you should also do."

Mick waited and about fifteen minutes later he heard someone enter his cabin, but it wasn't Callie, he could tell right away. He was surprised when the determined face of Taylor came into view at the top of the stairs.

"Taylor, what are you doing here?"

"You're a wolf man," he said simply.

"Did you see someone last night turn into a wolf?"

He shook his head. "I saw a lot of wolves and some naked people," he added with a look somewhere between disgust and curiosity. "Sammy is right, he does have a tail, doesn't he?"

"He will someday, yes, this is a wolf shifter pack."

"Werewolves? Are you guys going to bite me and my mom?"

"Not werewolves. They are made up stories. What we are is different and no, we don't bite, you can't turn into us."

Taylor looked disappointed but he came the rest of the way up the stairs and approached the bed. "I guess this means you really can protect me and mom."

"I want to, forever if she'll let me," he admitted. "Do you like the idea of staying here?"

"Oh yeah, this place is awesome!"

Mick smiled at the boy and felt a purr from his wolf, a desire to embrace him as pack. "Come here for a minute."

Taylor stepped cautiously forward. Mick reached out and ran a finger over the boys forehead and down one arm then embraced his hand. "There, now you smell like me and everyone will know you belong to this pack too."

Taylor seemed pleased with that and ran from the cabin with a whoop. Mick doubted his conversation with Callie was going to go as smoothly.

Half an hour later Callie came in. She'd obviously showered, her hair was still wet, and she'd braided it over one shoulder. She was beautiful in a pair of black biker shorts and a baggy T-shirt, no makeup. There was a band-aid on her knee and it made him frown and when he looked back up at her face he did his best to calm his features. He really wished she didn't have that frightened look behind her eyes, and that her body language didn't indicate she was about to run at the slightest indication he was angry. That thought was what kept his wolf on edge, the clear possibility that she was about to run.

He needed her to trust him.

"Did you eat or drink anything?" she asked from the top of the stairs, not coming fully into the room. "Tara said you wanted to talk to me, but I think you need to get your strength back first."

"That would be great, thank you," he said.

She disappeared back down the stairs and he listened to her move around his kitchen. The idea of her in his living space, touching his things, all in an effort to provide for him; it was a very intimate thing, and it pleased his base instincts. His wolf was practically purring as he listened.

When she reappeared, he was sitting up against the headboard and the blanket was pooled around his waist leaving his bare chest exposed. The way her eyes ran over the naked skin told him everything he needed to know about the possibilities of their relationship.

She was attracted to him too.

"That smells wonderful," he said with a low growl that had her stiffening slightly and he had to remind himself that she wasn't ready, that he didn't have her trust yet.

"It's just a sandwich and soup. You start eating and I'll go grab some water." Avoiding eye contact she set the tray on his lap and scurried from the room. She returned with the water and then looked anxious. He didn't have any chairs in the room, and she looked like she wanted to leave.

"Come sit while I eat, then we'll talk." He indicated the bed.

She hesitated, then sat gingerly on the foot of the bed, perched just slightly as if she were only putting half her weight down. Staying ready to bolt at the slightest indication of his anger.

He couldn't wait for the time when she would come to him with an eager smile and ask for all the things he could do to her. He could imagine once she was relaxed and trusting she would make the most amazing noises as he pleasured her. He wanted to make her grip the headboard and scream into pillows, he wanted to ... *fuck* ... he was thankful for the tray that was hiding his now very obvious erection under the blanket.

"Tell me why you were in the clubhouse," he demanded, needing a distraction.

She looked down and twisted her hands in her lap.

"I'm not angry, I'm just curious. I thought it would be the safest place for me to be so I could keep away from you while you didn't know what I was. But then there you were," he laughed.

CALLIE

Callie took a deep breath, not sure if she was ready to hear about what she saw but she also knew she needed to. She stared at her hands so she wouldn't ogle his chest which was deliciously exposed right now and reminded her of the rest of him which she'd seen last night.

"The kids wanted to roast hot dogs and marshmallows, so I went to the clubhouse looking for what we needed. I went downstairs because I thought there might be more down there, I knew that's where the extra supplies were kept, even though I'd never been down there," she huffed a little laugh. "I guess I know why."

"I didn't want you to see the cage and freak out thinking it was something weird."

She looked at him with shock. "Weird like a wolf human thing," she said, waving her hand at him.

He grimaced. "Yeah, weird like that."

"Will you tell me about it? Can you tell me or is it like a national secret?"

"I can tell you, but you can't tell anyone."

"Oh, I'll keep Taylor from figuring it out." Shit, was it too late?

Was this one of those, I could tell you but then I'll have to kill you, sorts of situations?

"Taylor already knows."

Fear sliced through her and she had an urge to bolt. "Don't worry, I won't let him tell anyone. I swear he won't he's just a kid he—"

"Stop," he snarled, and she cowered.

She hated that she cowered, but she did.

"Fuck, this is not going well." Mick moved the still mostly full tray off his lap and she grabbed it.

Thankful for an excuse to move, she fled the room with it.

She stood at the kitchen counter and stared outside. She watched people, young and old, walking around with smiles, chatting and laughing. She wondered if they were all like him, was everyone here some kind of animal person? If she bolted right now from Mick's cabin would they chase her down for him? She felt trapped and panic tightened her throat.

Then she saw Taylor. He skipped by the window with a group of kids, all of them happy and all of them treating him so well. They couldn't be bad, these people who had taken her and Taylor in, who had offered her a place to stay, food, and a job, who were fixing her car ... although she had a feeling there was more to that story than Lance was letting on seeing as he'd fixed it last night so quickly. But still, no one had harmed her or Taylor and last night —well, last night if Mick was telling the truth, he'd been trying to protect her, from himself.

Her eyes looked up at the loft and she wondered what the whole story was, and she knew she was scared, she knew she was probably making a mistake, but she needed to know it all before she left.

She gathered her courage and went back upstairs. He looked relieved when he saw her return and it settled her further.

"Is there anything else I can get you?" she asked.

"Sit down, Callie. This conversation is *not* over," he ordered, and she obeyed, sitting on the foot of the bed again.

"As I was trying to say. It's fine that you know, Taylor too," he hurried to say. "Me, and everyone else who lives here is a wolf shifter and the bear you shot that was attacking me, that was a bear shifter from a clan south of here that had come to stir up trouble. It's good you killed him because he would have killed us both then headed for the kids if you hadn't."

Everything he said terrified her and she stared at the floor for a minute digesting it. Somehow it made sense in a way she couldn't explain and she turned her head slowly to look at him with this new knowledge. "And you're in charge, you're their alpha? Is that a real thing?"

He nodded and she thought she saw relief pass over his face and his shoulders relax a bit. "Yes, that's it exactly."

"How did you—do they—or ... I guess, what are you? What is this, some kind of virus?"

"No, it isn't like the movies. This is what we are, a different species, so close to humans but not quite. We are born this way, when puberty hits, we start to change."

"And last night was a full moon, that's why you went camping?"

"Yeah, I wanted everyone away from you, not because they are dangerous, but because I didn't want to risk you seeing anyone before I had a chance to tell you."

"But why were you in the cage? Did you think you were going to hurt me?" she asked and her voice quivered, unable to forget the way he'd thrown himself against the cage, broken out of it and chased her.

"No, it's not like that. I was afraid," he paused and took a breath. "I was afraid of something else. When you were down there, I smelled the bear. The scent was so strong on you. That's what got my wolf freaked enough to bust out and I wasn't chasing you to harm you. I was trying to protect you from the bear, but my wolf is too strong during the full moon and I couldn't get back in control so I could actually talk to you."

She met his gaze and although she knew there was still something he was hiding; she felt the truth in his explanation.

"I'm sorry I scared you, Callie, that's the last thing I ever want to do."

"I'm sorry I shot you, twice."

"Yeah, that was not great," he admitted with a frown and ran a hand over the bandage on his shoulder.

"You should rest and I'm going to help clean up the mess in the clubhouse so we can open for dinner if not lunch." She stood and wished she had an excuse to stay now that she was sure he wasn't angry with her.

"You aren't leaving?"

"Lance said my car is fixed," she admitted, and his eyes narrowed. "But I don't have enough money to get far, especially after I pay him. I don't know what he's charging me for all the work he's done."

That answer didn't seem to satisfy Mick. "You still plan to leave though, when you can? To where?" he demanded.

She let out a frustrated laugh. "I have nowhere to go but I just know that I'm not safe unless I can get as far from Maine as possible."

"I will keep you safe, Callie. There's not a force on this earth that can harm you if I'm around."

She felt the strength in his statement and she wanted to believe it was true, but it didn't seem like enough. Why would he help her, protect her? And for how long? "I appreciate your willingness to help me and Taylor, I'm basically a stranger that got thrust into your life." She turned and hurried down the stairs before he could say anything else. She could see it burning in his eyes, a fierce denial to her assertion that she was nothing more than a stranger among his pack.

"Fate thrust you into my life because you're my wolf's perfect mate. There's nothing I wouldn't do to protect you" he said, just loud enough for her to not be sure she heard it correctly as she walked out the front door and closed it behind her.

Lance was sitting on the porch steps as if he'd been waiting for her. Callie sat next to him in silence for a few minutes. They watched the kids run around and play, happy and carefree. It was everything a kid deserved to have, and she loved that Taylor was getting it finally. She couldn't imagine taking him away from here, but just because Taylor was happy, it didn't mean they were safe.

"Did he tell you?" Lance asked finally.

"He told me what you all are, and I guess I am trying to wrap my head around it, but in a weird way it makes sense."

"And did he tell you why he chased you last night?"

"Because he smelled the bear; he was protecting me," she said.

Lance grunted as if he weren't satisfied with that answer. "You're staying?"

"How much do I owe you for fixing my car?" she asked.

"How much will it take for you to not be able to leave?" he countered.

She laughed despite his serious tone. "I'm staying, for now. At least to make sure Mick recovers. I'm certainly responsible for that, I just don't know how long before it won't be safe for us here and I don't want to bring trouble for anyone else. I don't know if this is far enough from Maine to keep Taylor safe."

"You think we would ever let anything happen to you or Taylor, Callie?" he asked, his face shocked. "Christ woman, we would literally jump in front of a bear for you. You're pack whether you want to be or not and I hope you can understand what that means." Lance got up and walked inside, leaving her just as confused as ever.

CHAPTER 16

KODY

Kody sighed heavily as the last ember of the funeral pyre went out, he watched the last of the smoke spiral into the night and he said one final goodbye to his brother.

He was exhausted. He went back to his trailer, showered and fell onto his bed. When he woke up the next morning it was with the knowledge that he was in charge of this pack now.

And there were some changes he needed to make immediately.

When he stumbled out of his bedroom one of those changes was sitting on his couch uninvited.

"Kody! Babe, oh my god, I heard about Kyr and I came right away."

"Why?"

Janet flipped her red hair and gave him a pouty face. She was dressed in a minimal sundress and her fingers were tugging up the hem to an indecent level. "I wanted to comfort you, of course."

"You want to fuck an alpha," he snarled.

"You know that's not all I'm after, babe," she said in a voice that might have made some men's blood rush south but it just left him cold.

"Not interested, now get out. I have shit to do."

"Like sniff around that bitch, Tara? Lot of good that will do when I tell her that you visited Allen the morning of the little *incident*. That he was so fucked up because you told him that you were coming for his woman and he needed to step out of the way. Do you think your little bitch princess is going to want you then? When she knows your macho asshole display is the reason she almost died?"

Kody snarled at Janet but he didn't answer. She was right, Tara would never forgive him if she knew he had gone behind her back to try and get Allen to back off, that he was the reason Allen had reacted so strongly that day. Kody had only wanted to rattle Allen and make him back off or act too possessive so that Tara would freak out on him and leave because she would never put up with that shit from a human.

He never thought the man was capable of such violence against the woman he claimed to love.

"That's what I thought," Janet sneered. "Well, I'll be ready for that date whenever you are, big boy," she said with a wink and left the trailer. "Just don't make me wait too long," she shouted as the door closed.

"Fuck!" Kody roared and slammed his hand through the closet door.

With a bloody hand he picked up his phone and stared down at Tara's number. He should tell her, right now, get it over with and deal with the consequences.

He collapsed onto the couch and dropped the phone on the floor between his feet, staring down at it with fear. He couldn't, there had to be another way.

TARA

When Callie walked into the cabin, Tara was nervous, ready to be looked at like a monster; ready to help the poor woman pack up and leave.

She wasn't ready for the questions.

Callie asked her a hundred, some very personal, questions about being a wolf shifter and shifting and even sex. And because she loved her brother, Tara answered them all as best she could all while vowing to punch him as soon as he was healthy for putting her through this.

"You're not too freaked out by it all?"

"No, what about the guy who I ... last night, so there are bears too?"

Tara nodded. "Kyr was the alpha, their clan is south of here and Kody, I guess, is alpha now."

"Oh! What is that look?"

"What look?" Tara defended.

"When you said *Kody* you had a look, I know that look, there's something there between you two."

"I guess."

"So, what's the problem? Didn't you say he saved you when you were attacked by your boyfriend?"

Tara bit her lip and closed her eyes, she hated to admit this, but Callie had told her so much personal stuff, she couldn't hold back. "I'm afraid of him."

"Did he hurt you? Mick will kill him," Callie said fiercely.

Tara's defenses sprang up immediately for Kody. "No, he's always been great, a perfect gentleman actually, it's just that, I've seen what he can do."

Tara told her everything then, how she'd watched Kody rip through Allen, how he'd looked and sounded and how she'd had nightmares for months afterwards about Kody, not Allen. It was hard to admit, but she was afraid of that power.

"I know he'd never use it against me, but it's there."

"I get it," Callie said softly. "Knowing what Mick is capable of … it's intimidating after what we've been through."

"But you can't think less of Mick for that, you know he would never, could never, turn violent with you, he sees you as his mate to protect and cherish, he'd rather bite off his own arm than harm you."

"And isn't that how Kody sees you?" Callie asked.

Tara narrowed her eyes at Callie. "Tricky woman."

"Well, I think we might just be in very similar situations is all, if you think I'm safe with Mick, maybe you're safe with Kody."

"Yeah, I had started to think that too, actually."

Chapter 17

Mick

Mick spent two days recovering, though he was fine after one, because Callie came by three times a day to feed him and talk with him and Taylor stopped in at least once a day to ask him questions and be reanointed with his scent, because he was sure his mother making him shower and him jumping in the lake washed it off and he wanted to belong. Mick was happy to oblige and each time he did, his wolf purred with pleasure at the pack's acceptance of this boy as theirs.

He kept conversations light with Callie. She talked about her childhood growing up in Maine and how her parents were older and died when she was in her twenties. She had no siblings, and she missed her parents every day. She didn't talk about Oliver or what being married to him had been like, but she didn't need to. Mick understood and wished he could reach into her brain and scoop out those memories for her so she'd never have to be reminded of her fear again. Also, so she wouldn't cringe or cower at noises or sudden movements ever again.

Every time she did it, which was getting less and less often, he wanted to rage, but he knew that any anger he showed, even if it wasn't toward her, only made her more fearful. So he had to hold himself back. He was building trust, but it was a slow process.

He told her about the history of the pack and his childhood, but only the good stuff. He told her how excited the pack was to find this place after moving around so much and how the bears were trouble from the start and the northern wolf pack wasn't much more welcoming.

"Is that why she was here that morning?"

Mick didn't need to hear Janet's name to know that's who Callie was talking about. He didn't want to talk about her, or what Callie had seen and heard that first morning, but he knew he needed to clear all the air with her if he was going to get her trust.

"Yes, I was supposed to marry her to join the packs, gain their support and keep the bear clan back."

"What happened that day?"

Callie deserved the truth no matter how it painted him in her eyes so Mick took a deep breath and dove in. "She was challenging me, her wolf coming out. It was baiting me by threatening you, and I lashed out to make her stop before she went too far. She needed to stop and understand before taking things to a point where one or both of us could have gotten seriously injured, especially with her father and Lance in the room. She could have started a war with her little tantrum. She needed to know that I wasn't going to be threatened or pushed into marrying her. I didn't harm her, but I had to get my point across to her the only way a wolf understands, force and dominance. You saw her, Callie. She walked out unharmed and angry, not scared and hurt aside from her pride. I'd rejected her, and she wanted to make sure you knew the worst about me."

Callie nodded but she wouldn't look at him and it killed him to know this could be the final straw, so he spoke without thinking. "So our date was postponed; want to go tonight?"

She looked up in surprise. "Are you up for that?"

"Definitely. Wolves heal very fast. Bridgette came by to check my wounds this morning, I'm fine to resume normal activities."

"Oh well, Taylor—"

"Will be fine with Tara. You aren't backing out on me, are you? I mean, you shot me twice and I still want a date, that's got to count for something," he said with a grin, hoping to remind her that he wasn't only a terrifying beast.

Callie laughed and his heart soared. He'd never heard a sound so beautiful and the way it lit up her face was magical. He wanted to spend the rest of his life making her laugh.

"Okay, I guess I owe you one."

"Technically, you owe me two," he said with a grin that she returned, and his heart melted some more.

It wasn't just his wolf that wanted her in his life forever.

"Meet me at the clubhouse at seven. We'll ride my bike to town and eat, wear something warm for the ride."

"Okay," she agreed and left with a look on her face he wasn't sure meant all good things.

CALLIE

Callie couldn't believe she'd agreed to a date, two maybe, had she agreed to two? It was all so confusing when she was with him. He made her feel things she didn't think she could feel and at the same time she was terrified of what he could do to her. How easily he could hurt her.

She distracted herself with work; serving and cleaning and basically not stopping moving, until it was six thirty and she wasn't clean or dressed for a date. She knew she needed to cancel because she was going to have a nervous breakdown just thinking about it. Partially because she wanted it so badly and anything she wanted so bad had to be dangerous. She'd wanted Oliver badly too, all those years ago. She had gone against her mother's and her friends' advice and married him. Look how that turned out. He'd broken her trust, her body, and her spirit.

She was terrified to give someone the opportunity to do that again.

She knocked at Mick's office door.

"Yeah," he called out.

She opened the door and walked in, hating herself for what she was about to do. He smiled as she entered but quickly dropped into a frown when he took in her nervous face.

"Can you close the door so the whole pack doesn't hear you canceling on me?" he snarled.

She cringed and closed the door. She walked to the front of the desk and gave him a pleading look. "I'm just not ready, Mick. I'm just not ready to give you what you're asking for."

"What exactly am I asking for, Callie?" he demanded. He stood and walked around the desk until he stood between her and the door.

She didn't like that, there was no escape, and she backed up until her legs were pressed against the desk. "You want a date; I don't know what else, but it's all so complicated. I have Taylor, and I can't just start seeing men. Christ, I'm still married!"

"What *men*?" Mick snarled, and she cowered. "Fuck," he breathed and stepped back, giving her the space she needed but still standing between her and the door. "Okay, I can give you time if that's what you really need."

"It is," she said, relaxing.

He turned and walked to the door. He had one hand on the knob when he spoke again. "I just wish you would trust me," he said sadly.

It broke her heart, and she wanted to cry hearing how vulnerable those words were. "I want to, Mick. I really do."

He opened the door and stood aside to let her out. "Come back when you do."

It might have been a moment of insanity, but she didn't move, didn't run. She stared at him, looking at the wall and waiting for her to walk out, offering to wait until she was ready. No anger, no abuse and no demands. Just opening his heart and soul and asking her to give him a chance.

"Help me," she whispered.

He looked at her, confused.

"Help me trust you, Mick. I'm so fucking broken. I don't even know how to fix this," she admitted, tears welling up in her eyes.

He pushed the door shut and walked over to her slowly, giving her every chance to tell him to stop or to push around him and leave the room. He grasped her face gently in his hands and stared into her eyes. "You aren't broken, Callie. You are perfection." He kissed her, his lips soft at first then when she parted hers slightly, he became demanding, slipping in his tongue and sweeping through her mouth with eagerness. She moaned and he pulled her body against his.

She thought she could get lost in his kiss and when his hands moved from her face to her shoulders, down her arms and then grasped her hands, she knew she was already lost to this man.

And that was a new kind of terrifying.

He kissed her jaw and her neck then up to her ear, nipping gently at her lobe. "I want you, Callie. I want every part of you, but I am trying to do this right. So please, go get changed and let me take you out on a date."

She nodded because words were lost in the haze of desire he'd ignited in her.

"Good girl," he growled and stepped away, dropping her hands and smiling like she'd just promised him the world.

Callie wasn't sure she was doing the right thing, but she *was* sure she wanted to find out. She hurried to Tara's cabin and took a speed shower, just washing off the day's sweat and kitchen smell. She wished she had something nice to wear on a date, but she was going to be on the back of his bike, so jeans made sense anyway. She hadn't packed anything date-worthy, she'd hardly packed anything at all. She threw on her cleanest T-shirt which was a light pink one with a little hole at the hem that she decided she could hide by tying it in what she hoped was a stylish cute way, but she wasn't sure she really pulled it off. Then she brushed her hair, braiding it so that she'd be able to keep it neat on the ride and touched up the little makeup she wore.

"This will have to be good enough," she grumbled.

"You could wear anything, and my brother would be panting," Tara said from the doorway, making her jump.

"I didn't hear you come in."

"That's because you were thinking too hard about how you look, you know he isn't concerned with your clothes, right?"

"I know, I just wish I had something a little more date-like. This is what I wear every day."

Tara looked her up and down and nodded. "You could borrow something from me if you want. I don't think any of my pants will fit you, since you're so damn skinny, but I have lots of cute tops."

"Oh, no you don't have to—"

"Just come on," Tara said, rolling her eyes and walking out of the room.

Callie followed her upstairs and was surprised to find Tara's loft bedroom was a complete disaster. She kept the cabin so clean, seeing this unorganized chaos was shocking. There were piles of clothes everywhere, some obviously brand new with tags still on and shoes too, a whole wall of them, everything from boots for hiking to stiletto heels.

"Don't judge me, I like to shop," Tara said.

"I'm not judging. I might be jealous though," Callie admitted.

Tara dug through a pile then held up a black long sleeve top with an incredibly low neckline and cut out patches on the arms.

"That looks too fancy, just a clean T-shirt without holes would be great."

"Don't even start, put it on," Tara threw the shirt at her then went back to digging.

Callie pulled her T-shirt off and the long sleeve on, it fit snug, hugging her small curves and revealed a decent hint at her breasts, the cut-out sleeves gave the otherwise casual cotton top a sexy flair that made her feel like she really *was* going on a date. And that made her heart start to pound.

"You'll need a jacket too," Tara said, holding up a red leather one.

"Oh, that's gorgeous."

"And always was a little snug on me so it should fit you perfectly."

Callie took the jacket and hugged Tara. "Thank you, will you tell Taylor that I'll kiss him goodnight when I get back?"

"Sure thing, we will watch movies and eat ice cream and won't even worry if you don't get back before the sun rises," she assured Callie with a wink.

"Tara, can I ask you a question," Callie said, suddenly nervous.

"Of course you can. What's on your mind?" Tara sat on her bed, pulling her legs up and stared at Callie expectantly.

Callie couldn't look at the woman as she asked the question on her mind. "Is there anything I should worry about? Like, I don't know, any customs or things ..." Callie trailed off.

"Like is he going to sniff your ass to make sure it's you?" Tara asked with a raised eyebrow and quirk of her lips.

"Never mind, thanks for the clothes," Callie huffed and turned.

"Hey!" Tara called out, stopping her. "Mick's a good guy, he won't hurt you, though he is a bit intense at times. We all are. It's part of our instincts."

Callie nodded, that made sense.

"I've dated humans before, there's nothing different about them except they don't get the cool ability to turn into a wolf and howl at the moon. You don't have to worry about a date."

"Thank you," she said, a little relieved. It was just a date, she knew she was freaking out for nothing. People went on dates all the time.

CHAPTER 18

MICK

Mick was waiting for her in front of the clubhouse and when she walked up he devoured her with his eyes. Tight jeans and a tight black shirt hinting at her perfect body underneath. She'd gained weight since being here and he loved to see it. She was so beautiful, and he wanted to skip the date. He wanted to take her back to his cabin and claim her, mark her. But he also wanted her to stick around after, wanted her to understand that this was the beginning of a forever relationship, not a fling, not just a date.

So he would take it slow, at least for tonight.

"Ready?" he asked, holding out a helmet.

"I guess so, I've never been on one of these before."

"Well, I am happy to be your first," he said with a wink.

She rolled her eyes and slipped the helmet on. He stepped forward to buckle it for her, then helped her into the jacket, zipping it up. It was a warm night, but the ride would be cooling and there was safety in layers that a very delicate human like her needed.

Once she was bundled, he got on the bike and helped her to settle behind him. She was trying to keep her distance and he wasn't going to allow that. He reached back and pulled her forward until her body was pressed snug against him. "Wrap your arms around me and just let your body move with mine."

She slid her arms around him tentatively. He started the bike, the roar of the engine disguising the grumble of approval his wolf let out at her close and intimate position.

They took off and she held on tighter, gasping as he sped down the road. After a couple minutes she relaxed slightly, and he knew she was finding out how wonderful the back of a bike could be. It was a freeing experience unlike any other and he had never been happier to share it with someone.

He took the road that followed along the river, it was a little longer, but it was so beautiful and he wanted to show her what a wonderful place this was to stay. She relaxed behind him and he hoped it was because she was taking in the scenery. His wolf wanted to believe it was all him. She was relaxing because he was in complete control here and she was accepting that, accepting them. Mick didn't bother trying to convince his wolf any different which led to a lot of blood pooling in his crotch. He could feel the heat of her body behind him and her arms and hands wrapped around his front. Even through all the layers of clothing he could feel the burn of her and it stoked the fire in his veins and his eyesight sharpened as his wolf tried to take more control from him.

When they got to the small town of Millsburg he parked in front of a little Mexican restaurant and sat for a moment to force his wolf back, and will his cock down.

Callie didn't move immediately either and he hoped it was because she was enjoying the close contact as much as he was. After he was sure his body was under control, he patted her hands and turned the bike off.

"You survived, I hope it wasn't too bad," he said, turning to look at her.

She was smiling, her eyes bright and her cheeks a little red from the wind that had slipped under the visor.

"That was amazing!"

He laughed and unbuckled her helmet. "I think so too." He couldn't resist pulling her in for a kiss, he didn't linger but made sure she felt his desire in it, and he felt hers too. It pleased his wolf.

Dinner was going great, just as he'd known it would. This was his favorite place to eat away from the pack and enjoying it with Callie brought it to a whole new level. As if seeing her pleasure in something he liked and was so familiar with, was a step in the direction of becoming one. A prelude to the rest of their lives when they would know each other's quirks, likes, and dislikes. He couldn't wait to be so familiar with her that he would guess her needs before she had them, and provide for everything before she wanted for a thing. He couldn't imagine anything better, and he hoped she would understand what doing those things for her was going to mean to him, how it would please his wolf to be the provider, protector, and the one who knows her the most intimately.

They were about halfway through the meal when his senses went on alert. His head whipped to the door, and he let out a low growl.

Janet walked into the restaurant on the arm of a bear shifter, Brandon. If Mick remembered right, this was Kyr's best friend which could be a problem.

"Is that—" Callie asked, following his gaze to the door and focusing on Janet.

"It is," Mick snarled, "fuck."

"Should we leave?"

"No, this is neutral territory, the family that runs it is all witches. Janet and Brandon would be idiots to make trouble here." He narrowed his eyes at them. What the hell was a bear shifter doing with Janet anyway?

Janet glowered his way and pressed her body against Brandon's large form. She looked like she'd shrunk her dress but wore it anyway. It barely covered her ass, and her boobs were popping out the top. Brandon glared back, looking like he was struggling to control his anger, and it was directed at Callie.

Mick growled, low and menacing.

Esmerelda, the restaurant owner appeared just then, defusing the situation. She was a small, grandmotherly type with graying hair and only about five feet tall on a good day, but she packed a lot of magic, and she wasn't afraid of wolves or bears. She looked way up at Brandon and poked a bony finger up in his face.

"You don't make trouble in my house," she ordered.

Brandon looked at Mick then back to her and nodded.

"Fine, then go eat." She didn't acknowledge Janet, probably assuming Brandon would keep his date in line.

Mick hoped she was right.

As the old woman walked away, her granddaughter, Helena, led the couple to the only empty table in the place, which was uncomfortably close to Mick and Callie's.

Mick tried to ignore them and keep the date going but the conversation between him and Callie became flat and empty. He didn't want to discuss anything meaningful within those two's earshot, and honestly he was trying to listen to theirs. All he caught was Janet's constant prattling on about how attractive and strong and wonderful Brandon was, and fishing for compliments for herself which Brandon just grunted about, not bothering to try and converse at all.

Mick wasn't sure it was a date they were on, but it seemed Janet at least wanted it to seem like one. If anything, Mick was willing to bet it was a booty call and he wondered if her father knew she was sleeping with bear shifters. It certainly hadn't been revealed to him in the early discussion of marriage to the woman. He'd heard about her dalliances with the wolves in her pack and some humans from town, but no bears. Maybe this was new, but somehow he doubted it.

"Do you want to leave?" Callie whispered and brought Mick's attention back to her.

He realized she'd stopped eating and was sitting, staring at him while he paid no attention to her.

"No, sorry, I want to finish our dinner," he assured her.

She didn't look convinced and gave the other table a nervous glance before beginning to eat again.

The rest of dinner was ruined. With almost no conversation between him and Callie, she became more and more uncomfortable. When she excused herself to use the restroom he paid the check, then waited for her at the door eager to get away from this place. When she came out of the bathroom she looked relieved to be leaving, and he hated that this experience had been anything but perfect for her.

"Oh, my purse," she said and hurried back to the table for the bag he hadn't even realized was sitting under it.

"Can you believe that's the twit that shot and killed your alpha," Janet said as Callie scooped the bag up.

"You're a bear," Callie whispered, making the connection he'd intentionally left unsaid.

Callie froze as Brandon turned his dark eyes to her and growled low and menacing.

Mick's instincts kicked in and he was across the room in one leap, his body already rippling with the need to shift. If it wasn't for the spell on the place that inhibited shifting, he'd have wolfed already.

Just as his arms wrapped around Callie to pull her to safety, Brandon stood, knocking over the table of food and splattering Janet with salsa and beans. Esmerelda charged out of the back waving her hand and demanding they stop immediately and get out.

Mick didn't have to be told twice, he hauled Callie off the ground and straight out the front door. He dropped her on the bike and put her helmet on then jumped on in front of her and tore out of the parking lot. He wasn't taking any chances where she was concerned and the look of murder in Brandon's eyes was undeniable.

He rode fast and took the shorter route back to his pack's territory. If it was just him, he'd have happily stayed and fought the bear in Callie's defense, but he knew he couldn't have her around that kind of violence again, not if he wanted any chance to convince her he was a safe place for her and Taylor.

A hope that might already be out the window.

CALLIE

Callie was shaking, adrenaline coursing through her body and when Mick pulled off the road she couldn't even make herself get off the bike. She wasn't sure where they were, this wasn't the clubhouse and that made her nervous.

"Callie?" Mick asked as he gently removed her helmet. "Callie, talk to me. Are you alright?"

She blinked and looked up at him, his face was full of concern and care, there was a slight yellowing to his eyes that she was unsure of but other than that, he looked like he really was just worried about her. She clung to that.

"I killed that man's friend," she whispered, speaking the horrible truth. It was one thing to know she'd killed in defense of herself, it was another to see the people left behind.

She'd done that and there was no taking it back. To that man, she would always be a monster and the thought made her sick.

"Oh, babe," Mick said and wrapped his arms around her.

He was so warm, so firm, and she loved it. She didn't know if this was where she was going to find safety forever, but she did know that it's where she felt right in this moment, and she clung to that. She pressed her lips to his neck and felt him shudder, then she opened her mouth and drew his musky skin in and he howled. His hands moved from her back to grip her ass and he pulled her tight against him so she could feel his hard cock.

"Do that again and I won't be able to stop myself from taking you right here on the side of this road, Callie," Mick said with a husky growl in his voice that made her shiver with desire.

She wondered how close he was to the edge of his control. She took a moment to consider that and how she really felt.

Was she afraid of him? No, she really wasn't and if Tara and Lance were to be believed, she had no reason to be because he wouldn't, or couldn't, hurt her.

She didn't trust her voice, so she nipped at his earlobe instead. She didn't want him to stop right now.

The growl that he released was so menacing she was sure she heard things scamper away in the nearby underbrush. But it didn't frighten her, didn't make her want to scurry. It sent a thrill of heat through her body and made her even more desperate to feel his skin against hers.

His hands moved from her ass as he bent his head to capture her lips in a penetrating kiss. Fingers and hot palms roamed her body, up her hips and to her stomach then slipped under her coat and pushed it off of her. She only then realized that her own hands were clasped desperately in his shirt as if she were afraid he was going to walk away and leave her in this state of painful need. She let go as his hands ran down her arms, removing the jacket. Then his touch was back on her waist and this time he found skin. His hands ran higher and closed around her sides under her shirt.

Her body burned where he made contact and she moaned into his mouth, pressing her hips forward to encourage more. He took the hint with a groan, yanking at the button of her jeans and then pushing them roughly down, taking her lacy underwear with them. She felt exposed, the cool night air against her bare ass and she hesitated just a second until she felt his fingers reach between her legs, felt his finger easily slip through her folds and land with precision on her sensitive clit. She was lost at the first stroke. Her head fell back and her hands clutched his shoulders.

He groaned approval as she shuddered at his precise stroking.

"Oh, babe, you're so perfect," he growled and nipped at her neck. He lifted her and set her down on the bike, her bare ass perched on the edge of the leather seat. He kneeled in the dirt and looked up at her with yellow eyes and a serious set to his lips. He helped her the rest of the way out of her jeans and panties then pushed her knees wide.

She was tempted to close her legs when he inhaled deeply, obviously smelling her wet sex. It seemed so personal, so embarrassing. What the hell was he even doing?

"So perfect," he growled again and leaned forward, one hand on each thigh, he delved his tongue where his finger had been so expertly stroking her. She almost exploded off the bike. No one had ever—Oliver had never—done this, and although she'd read about it in books, the real thing was beyond words. She squirmed and her hands went to his hair, pulling him closer with abandon. She no longer cared what he might see or smell, or even taste. She didn't care that they were barely off the road and anyone could happen upon them. She was lost to his tongue, lips, and teeth and for the first time in her life she came without having done all the work herself.

As her body tried to collapse and she made noises that she'd never heard herself make before, Mick kissed his way up her body, pushing her shirt up as he went until he was at her breasts. He nipped at her nipples through her bra before moving all the way up. He pulled her shirt over her head but left it over her arms so her movements were restrained. Then he captured her mouth with his again, his hands on her back pulling her body close to his.

When he pulled back and looked into her eyes, she was dizzy, needy and lost to whatever he wanted to do to her. Never in her life had she felt so willing to be at someone else's mercy. But she knew that Mick was safe and capable. She *wanted* to give him all control.

"I want your taste in my mouth every day for the rest of my life," he growled and licked his lips.

Callie's cheeks reddened but she didn't look away, didn't want to hide from him.

"I need you to understand what's about to happen before we go any further," he said with a suddenly serious tone, his eyes intense and focused on her. His hands grasped her shoulders and she stiffened at the change in him, but she still didn't try to get away, didn't break eye contact.

His eyes were slightly yellow, something she'd come to realize was a sign of his wolf and the realization that this man before her was holding back a beast made her shiver. Fear iced through her but there was also desire and she couldn't decide which was going to win out.

"I am going to bury my cock inside you, I am going to take you to that edge again and I am going to love every second of feeling your body start to convulse around me like you just did against my tongue."

Callie nodded, biting her lip, unsure if he expected a response. What he was describing sounded like great sex, nothing to be worried about, nothing to be so serious about either.

"When you're coming, I am going to bite you, here," he said and touched her neck gently.

That didn't sound too odd, he'd already nipped at her neck, breasts and thighs, even her clit. So why would this be different?

"I have to leave a mark, my wolf demands it, Callie. Do you understand? This is your chance to stop me, this is your off ramp because if I let my wolf out to claim you, he'll never allow you to leave us."

Panic bubbled through her at his words, the idea of being trapped, being controlled and being in a situation like she'd just escaped—hadn't truly escaped if she were being honest. She couldn't do it, a part of her wanted to give in and say yes, let his passion continue and see where it would lead. Let this man and his pack be hers and Taylor's. But she couldn't, she couldn't make the same mistake twice.

"No," she whispered through a throat thick with emotion. He tore himself away so quickly she stumbled, her trapped hands tried to catch herself on the bike, burning her hand in the process. "Fuck!" she yelped.

"Damnit, Callie," Mick growled and grabbed her roughly and spun her around. She shrunk away at his anger, but he was only interested in inspecting her wound, not harming her further for her rejection.

"I'm sorry," she said with a sob, glad she couldn't see him.

"This isn't your fault," he growled, his voice harsh even if his words were nice and his hands gentle as he slid her shirt back up her arms and over her head. As soon as he let go of her shirt, she bent for her pants but he was faster, already kneeling and helping her. It was mortifying, her naked lower half at eye level with him after she'd just made him stop, knowing he'd had his head buried there, his tongue all over her and she'd come, but he hadn't. He'd stopped because she'd asked him to. But she knew she wasn't wrong to stop him, not when his words were so real. What would it even mean to be with someone like him? This wasn't her reality and as much as she wished she could throw caution to the wind and jump on the opportunity he presented, she knew that she'd be destroyed in his hands. If he treated her even half as controlling as Oliver had, she'd lose the little bit of herself she'd gained in the last weeks of working and living freely with Taylor.

She shivered at the graze of his knuckles on her skin as he pulled her panties and jeans up. She heard his chest rumble as he slipped over her still wet curls, his hands shaking slightly as he finished. Reaching her waist he zipped and buttoned then stepped back.

"We should get back," he said, more growl than words, his eyes yellow and frightening.

Callie wrapped her arms around herself. "Mick," she said, wanting reassurance, wanting to know that he didn't hate her. He met her gaze and she couldn't hold it, she looked away and down at her hand that was already blistering. "Yeah, we should go," she finished lamely as she slipped her shoes back on.

He got on the bike and she sat behind him, careful of her injured hand, she reached around him and he took off. It wasn't like before, his body was stiff, his pace was slower, and she knew she'd lost the chance for whatever he might have offered. But she'd had to, his offer felt far too familiar.

Oliver's words on their wedding night ran through her head *You're mine now, by law and in the eyes of God. I will do whatever I want, and you'll never leave me.*

Her young brain hadn't realized the intent behind the words, taking them as a declaration of love. It hadn't taken long for her to realize what they were.

A statement of ownership and a loss of all her control.

CHAPTER 19

MICK

"What the hell did you do?" Tara snarled, coming into Mick's cabin without knocking.

He'd gotten Callie back to the camp, slathered her hand with antibiotic cream and wrapped it with a bandage then sent her to Tara. He'd gone straight to his liquor cabinet and was on his third whisky. His wolf raged inside of him, remembering the taste of her and howling his displeasure at being denied his chosen mate. All Mick could do was drink and hope that the memory of her on his tongue would fade someday.

"I told her the truth."

Tara shook her head. "No, you scared the shit out of her, what the hell were you thinking trying to fuck her in the woods like an animal."

His eyes shot to his sister. "Is that what she told you?"

"No, she didn't have to. I could smell it on her. She smelled like arousal and your wolf but not sex, plus she's not marked, so she made you stop, didn't she?"

Mick shook his head. "She had to know what she was getting into, what would happen if I let the wolf claim her."

"And?"

"She denied him. She rejected me," he said sullenly and shot back the rest of what was in his glass.

Tara grabbed the bottle before he could pour another one. "And you're just giving up?"

"What do you want me to do? Force her?"

"No, but you know you could have explained things better. The girl thinks you want to lock her in a basement. After what she just ran from, do you really think your explanation was comforting?"

Mick growled at his sister. He wasn't sure what Callie had confessed to her, but it was obviously her worst interpretation of the situation.

"I told her the truth, Tara. That my wolf won't let her go if he claims her physically."

"Yeah, but did you also tell her that the claim puts her in complete control of the wolf? That she can order it to do anything even against *your* will? Did you explain that you are offering to give over complete control to *her*?"

Mick looked away, knowing he hadn't.

"That's what I thought. You just told her the part that would make her run. Do you want her to leave, Mick? What are you so afraid of?"

Mick glared at her because he knew she was well aware of what his problem was, what he was afraid of.

"She's not our mother and *you're* not our father, but if you let her go, you'll die desperate and alone, likely by Lance's hand or mine. Fuck, Mick, don't put that shit on us."

With those parting words Tara walked out of his cabin still holding his bottle.

Mick glared at the door, debating what to do next, hating that Tara's words were right. He stormed out and stripped as he headed for the woods. He shifted and howled, then, as he did so many nights, he sat in the shadows outside the bedroom window where he knew Callie and Taylor slept.

The window was cracked to let in the night air and he could hear her talking quietly.

"Go back to sleep, Taylor, it's late."

"Did you have fun with Mick? Tiffany said you're going to marry him and then I'll be special because my dad will be the ruler of the pack. Will I be able to turn into a wolf then too?"

Callie didn't say anything for a while and Mick imagined her frowning as she tried to think of what to say to her young son.

"I don't plan to marry anyone, and you don't need a dad to be special, Taylor."

"I think he'd be a good dad, and I don't think he would hurt you, Mom."

"No, he wouldn't hurt me," she said, and Mick could hear the *but* in her tone. He wouldn't hurt her, *but* he would keep her, control her, and rule her life the same as Oliver had for so many years.

She sighed heavily. "Now go back to sleep."

Mick listened, knowing she was slipping into bed as well and he ached to be there, with her and with Taylor. To protect and love them. But he was haunted by the relationship his parents had.

Lance walked up to stand near him, arms crossed over his chest. "Walk with me," he said and turned to go deeper into the woods.

Mick didn't want to move away from Callie, but he couldn't ignore his pack over a woman who'd rejected him. He shifted to human form, his wolf reluctant to give up control but the moon wasn't full, and Mick was well in charge.

"I take it things didn't go well?" Lance said.

"Not what I had planned at all," Mick admitted.

"Well, I don't think you're going to like what I have to tell you."

Mick narrowed his eyes at his second and let his wolf yellow his eyes. "What?" he demanded.

"Esmerelda called. Apparently, Callie left her purse at the restaurant in all the confusion, and she'd put it aside for you, but later she realized it was gone. What are the chances it was just some random pickpocket, and not a slighted wolf shifter and her bear shifter plaything?"

"Not likely," Mick snarled.

"What do you think she'll do with it?"

"Worst case scenario? Find out who Callie is and contact her husband, tell him where she and Taylor are." Mick's panic and need to protect them was nearly overwhelming. His instincts screamed to grab her and run.

But he couldn't, he barely had a right to care, she'd rejected him.

His wolf growled disagreement.

"I don't want her to worry, don't tell her anything and we'll just keep an extra careful eye out for trouble," Mick instructed. "I'd love him to try and come in here and touch either one of them."

"You know we'll protect them like our own," Lance said, then gave him a pitying look and walked away.

"She may be ours, but I want her to be *mine*," Mick muttered, and his wolf agreed.

He shifted and slunk back to his favorite spot to watch her darkened window. He was surprised to see her standing there and when her gaze landed on him in the shadows she stiffened. He didn't react, just sat and watched her, waiting to see what she might do.

She disappeared from the window after a moment, and then he heard the front door of the cabin open and close. He was about to go around and see what she was doing but she stepped around the cabin, a thin blanket wrapped around her, legs bare and no shoes on. If he hadn't been in wolf form, he would have frowned at the carelessness for her delicate feet's safety. He didn't move as she approached.

"You're Mick, or ... you're Mick's wolf?" she asked, stopping a few feet away.

His wolf head nodded.

"You think I'm your mate?"

He nodded again.

"Can I come close?" she asked, so quiet he would have missed it if he didn't have supernatural hearing. "Tara says you won't hurt me." She didn't sound confident.

He nodded and laid down to help her feel more comfortable.

She approached cautiously; her eyes glued to his face as if she expected him to lash out with sharp teeth at any moment. She stopped when she was close enough to reach out and she touched his head.

"So soft," she said with surprise.

He closed his eyes as her fingers ran through his fur and a rumble of contentment vibrated his chest. When she stepped away, he couldn't hold back a whine at the loss of contact. He sat up and looked at her, waiting to see what she might do next.

"You're not a terrifying monster, but that doesn't mean I can accept being owned by you," she admitted, looking down at her feet. "I'm sorry, Mick."

He moved slowly, approaching her and rubbing his head against her legs and side. He wanted to cover her in his scent. He moved lower, making sure to rub against her bare skin.

She giggled as his fur tickled across the back of her knees. "What are you doing?" she laughed.

He grunted and licked her calf.

She pushed him away with another laugh. "Okay, that's enough of that," she said, her voice stern but with a hint of mirth.

He sat obediently and looked up at her with innocent eyes.

"You're a good boy," she said then covered her mouth and

gasped. "Shit, sorry. I hope that's not offensive; I didn't mean to imply you're a dog, or a pet or ... anything."

He rolled his eyes and tilted his head hoping she'd understand that he wasn't offended, had in fact liked the interaction far too much. The wolf was practically preening at her attention.

"Goodnight, Mick," she said and walked away.

He waited until he heard the cabin door close then went back to his watch spot and settled in for the night.

KODY

Kody watched as Brandon returned from the date he'd forced the guy into. He walked up to the man's truck and the scent of Janet and sex wafted out of the cab.

"I guess it went well?" Kody asked, his nose curling up in disgust. It had been a risk, sending Brandon on the date that was supposed to be his, but he just couldn't bring himself to do it, not when he knew Tara would flip if she found out. His hope had been that Brandon would be enough of a distraction to the impulsive and conniving wolf, Janet.

"She's a good lay, enthusiastic," Brandon said with a wide grin. "After we ran into Mick and the fucking human who shot Kyr, I needed to let off some steam and she was more than willing."

Kody watched as Brandon's features shivered, his anger barely controlled.

"You know that Kyr was out of line, going into their territory and attacking a human."

"Sure, but those wolves shouldn't even be there, Kody."

Kody reached out and pushed one large paw onto Brandon's chest, shoving him back against his truck, his bear claws sprang out of his fingertips and pushed into Brandon's flesh slightly. "I'd be very careful what your next words are, Brandon. I am in charge now and the wolves are not the enemy."

Anger and resentment flashed through Brandon's eyes but he didn't react, he knew that he'd lose in a fight against Kody.

When Kody knew he had control, he dropped his hand, his claws retracting and turned to walk away.

"Oh, Janet said you still owe her," Brandon called out as Kody stalked off toward his trailer.

Of course she did ... he was going to have to figure out a way to deal with her.

"Hey."

The voice surprised him and he spun to find Ava standing half in shadow, arms wrapped around herself and staring at her feet. Her eye was almost healed up and he was glad to see no new bruising on the girl. He'd made it clear to her and her father that she was to be treated with respect by everyone in the clan and she wasn't going to be mated off unwillingly at any point. They'd wait for the mate bond to form with someone, in their clan or another.

"Do you need something?"

"I just wanted to say, thank you."

He grunted and turned to start walking again, he had done what any alpha should do, take care of his clan.

"I didn't want to mate with Kyr," she said, surprising him again with how quietly she'd gotten close behind him.

"You should have come to me about it from the start."

"You weren't in charge," she said with a shrug and looked away.

"I am now."

"I know, thank you. It's just that ..."

"What?" Kody demanded and regretted the roughness of his tone when she flinched.

"Everyone thinks I was throwing myself at Kyr and they look at me like they are waiting for me to throw myself at you."

"That's ridiculous—"

"No," she snapped interrupting him with her fierceness. "You don't understand. Kyr used me and he let," her jaw tightened and she looked away, "others too, and they are waiting to see what you'll allow. What you'll take from me. They don't believe that you ordered me to wait for a mate bond."

"Ava, you don't need to be afraid of that. I have no interest."

"That almost makes it worse, if I'm not yours," she stepped forward and dropped her arms revealing a nearly see-through top and no bra underneath. "Then they are going to try and take me, I'm not strong enough and my father doesn't think there's a better way. He doesn't believe mate bonds should matter while we are a dying species."

"Stop, Ava, I don't want you," he growled.

Fear filled her eyes and she took one step back. "Then how will you keep me safe?" she whispered desperately and ran away.

"Fuck!" he snarled and turned back toward his trailer, confused by the girl's actions. He found Laura watching him, leaned against his porch. "What do you want?"

"You're a good alpha, Kody. Everyone can see you're doing things right around here and that scares them because they liked the way things were. You are going to have to get that girl out of here or marry her to someone immediately."

"I know. It's one of the many problems I need to deal with."

"Want my advice on the others?"

"No."

"Well, you get it anyway. I know you think you fucked up. I know you blame yourself, but I don't think Tara will see it the same way. Just tell her. We aren't humans, we don't always understand or predict their reactions and the fact that you put out your intentions like any good shifter would, doesn't mean you did wrong. That insane man was wrong, Tara will know that."

"But what if she doesn't?" he said.

"You're not responsible for other people's actions, Kody."

"If I hadn't been there, if I hadn't cornered him that morning—"

"And if I hadn't been on a date I'd be dead along with the rest of my clan that got hunted down. Our choices affect everything from that point on, it's true, but that doesn't mean we have to let those choices destroy our future."

Kody went into his trailer and pulled out his cell. He opened his message thread with Tara. But just as he was about to send a text initiating a date knowing he'd tell her everything, Janet's name appeared as an incoming call.

"What?"

"Brandon's not as good in bed, you still owe me."

"I am not interested, why are you calling me?"

"Oh, you sound like you forgot what I know you did, be careful, I know Tara's phone number too."

"What do you want, Janet?"

"I came across some interesting information, seems like Mick's little human is on the run from a husband desperate to get her and their son back. I already made contact. I need you to help me make sure he gets his family back."

"You're insane, why would I do that? Mick would kill the human who tried to take his mate from him, and Callie obviously ran away for a reason."

"That's what I need some bear muscle for. To make sure he gets her and his kid."

"You're not thinking straight."

"Or I call Tara right now."

Kody knew he had to agree, if she told Tara before he could, he would never get her trust. "Fine."

"Wonderful, I'll get you the details when he comes to town."

Janet hung up and Kody stared down at his phone. What had he just done?

I need to meet you, now.

I can't, I'm on Northern patrol duty tonight.

Tomorrow?

Yeah, meet me for coffee?

Sounds good

Kody dropped the phone on the table and put his head in his hands. Tomorrow morning would determine the rest of his life. But he had something that needed to be dealt with tonight. He stalked out of his trailer in search of Ava because Laura was right. That girl needed to get out of this pack or she'd never be safe from what Kyr forced her to become.

Chapter 20

Callie

The next morning Callie woke with a start from dreams of cages and wolves and faceless men. Half of it was terrifying and the other half ... had her desiring to take everything Mick was offering her no matter the consequences.

The ache in her hand distracted her quickly. When she left the room she found Taylor in front of the television with a bowl of cereal and Tara sipping coffee in the kitchen while frowning down at her phone.

"Good morning," Callie said to Tara and kissed Taylor on the head.

"Morning. Coffee?"

"Please. Is everything okay?" she motioned to the phone Tara was gripping white knuckled.

"Yeah, just got cancelled on for a coffee date."

"Oh? Kody?"

"Yeah, said he had a clan emergency, something about getting a girl out of town."

"Well, sounds reasonable I guess."

Tara just shrugged and drank deeply from her coffee mug.

"I need to change this bandage first though I think."

"Oh, let me see," Tara said and set her cup down, holding out her hand for Callie's.

Callie laid her injured hand in Tara's and let the woman unwrap it. She carefully inspected the burn then slathered it with something that smelled awful but immediately started to ease the pain then rewrapped it.

"I think you'll live."

"Good," Callie laughed. "I've definitely survived worse," she added.

Tara frowned. "Yeah, you have," she said with a sigh. "Do you know you smell like Mick's wolf?" she asked as she handed her a cup of coffee. "Like, way worse than you did last night when you got back from the date."

"Oh, is that different than smelling like Mick?"

"Yeah," Tara laughed. "It is definitely different. Did he sneak in to check on you last night?"

Callie's cheeks reddened. "No, I saw him out the window and went to talk to him." She shrugged. "I don't know, I guess I wanted to see how scary he was up close when he wasn't attacking a bear, and I didn't have a gun pointed at him."

"And?" Tara prompted.

"He is intimidating for sure, so big I think he could fit my whole head in his mouth. But he just laid there while I touched him, he was gentle when he rubbed against me. I—I don't know, he was kind of cute I guess," Callie said, and her cheeks flamed. How ridiculous was it to call a wolf shifter cute?

Tara laughed. "Don't tell anyone else you think so, it'll ruin his reputation." Tara cocked her head. "Then again, you should spread that round like wildfire, it wouldn't hurt him to get knocked down a peg or two."

"I would never want to harm his reputation," she said with a wink. "I did call him a good boy last night though and he didn't seem to mind."

Tara grinned slyly, "No, I don't imagine he minded at all."

Callie spent the morning watching the kids play around the clearing then went to work at the clubhouse. She didn't see Mick, but she was sure he was near. There seemed to be a lot of the pack around actually, more than usual and she wasn't sure what was going on, but it made her uneasy. She was never alone, even as she prepped and cleaned for lunch there were more workers than usual and there were two men sitting on the front porch of the clubhouse all day just drinking coffee and chatting as if it wasn't unusual.

When Callie tried to ask Tara about it, she just shrugged and changed the subject.

The next day was the same. She saw Mick in passing and she saw him out her window at night, but he didn't seek her out to chat, didn't ask her on a second date, and didn't pressure her for anything. She appreciated it but she also wished he would. A part of her wanted him no matter the consequences. Maybe that was his plan, he was starving her of his presence so she'd take whatever he gave her, strings and all.

By the third day she couldn't stop herself from seeking him out. She knocked on his office door between the lunch and dinner rush.

"Yeah," he barked out sounding irritated enough that she hesitated.

She took a deep breath then walked into the office. He was sitting behind his desk, a tight black T-shirt showing off his strong tattooed arms and his hair was a mess as if he'd been pulling his hands through it. His eyes sparked yellow when she entered, and his lips clamped into a twist. She wasn't sure if it was a held back smile or scowl. He was so attractive, her body betrayed her, she could feel her nipples tighten and her thighs clench, remembering what he'd done to her on the side of that road. All other thoughts flew from her mind.

"What can I do for you, Callie?" he asked, his voice gruff and he sat forward, his eyes intense, she wondered if he could somehow tell where her mind was.

"Oh, um, yes ... I came in to tell you that we will need more whisky the next time you order."

"Lance does most of the liquor ordering, I handle the restaurant side."

"Oh, Okay, I'll let him know then." Embarrassed, she turned to make a quick exit.

"Callie," His voice stopped her, and she turned to find him standing close behind her.

"Mick," she breathed his name.

He lifted a hand and trailed a finger down her arm from her shoulder to her hand. "How is your burn doing?"

"Oh, it's okay, healing quickly, thanks for asking."

"I hate that I was the cause of any harm that came to you."

"It wasn't your fault," she said.

He lifted her bandaged hand, it really was almost completely healed, the bandage was only necessary because she didn't want to get any cleaning solutions on it while working. He pressed a kiss to the bandage, and she shivered.

"I would do anything to keep you safe."

"I know." And she did, she believed that statement with a hundred percent certainty, but at what cost? Her freedom?

"I want to take you out again."

"I don't know if that's a good idea."

"Why?" he asked, his voice soft but there was a pressure behind his words, a demand for an answer that will satisfy.

"Because I'm afraid I won't be able to tell you no a second time," she admitted.

He nodded and stepped back, dropping her hand. "You need more time to build up trust, I understand. Will you at least believe me when I tell you that it isn't what you think. That it's so much more and so much better?"

"I don't understand."

"I know and if I was a better man I'd explain it all but I—I can't. I guess I'm waiting to trust you enough too."

His words surprised Callie. Why would he need to trust her, unless he was worried she'd tell his secret and risk the pack's existence.

"I would never reveal your secret, I would never tell anyone about the existence of wolf or bear shifters," she laughed a little. "It's not like anyone would believe me anyway."

"No, I suppose they wouldn't."

Before anything else could be said Lance rushed into the office. "Madeline's in labor!"

"Should we get to the hospital?" Callie asked.

"No, she'll be fine at home, but she'll need her alpha," Lance explained.

Mick nodded, "I'm on my way."

Lance yelped in excitement and ran out. For such a large and intimidating guy, he was acting like a kid on Christmas, and it made Callie's heart happy, then sad. The day Taylor was born, Oliver couldn't be bothered to leave the bar where he was watching football. She'd been three hours with her infant son before he stumbled into the room smelling like alcohol and perfume, but what could she say? She was more vulnerable in that moment than any in her life as she looked down at the helpless little boy in her arms. She had no way to care for or protect him, so she'd ignored the obvious, as usual, and introduced Oliver to his son.

"Looks like your father," he'd griped and pinched her arm. "Why the hell doesn't he look more like me?"

Luckily a nurse came in then and Oliver had taken a seat while the nurse fussed over her and the baby and Oliver had fallen asleep by the time the nurse was leaving the room.

"Keep Taylor away from the house. The screaming could scare him," Mick said, pulling her out of her memories.

"Oh, okay, yeah we'll hang out here."

"Callie," he said and grabbed her hand, he looked unsure, his eyes flashing yellow. "We'll talk later."

"Of course," Callie said and then he was out the door. Callie walked out to the main room, and everyone was gone, a few minutes later Taylor ran in. "Madeline's having her baby and Mick said you were going to give me a treat!"

"Sure am," Callie said with a smile for her son and gave him a hug. No matter the circumstances that had brought this boy into her life, she wouldn't give him up for anything. "Sit there and I'll see what we have in back."

While Taylor ate pie and ice cream, Callie busied herself cleaning. Her thoughts on the wellness of Madeline and the new baby, as well as the conversation with Mick that had been interrupted.

When the front door flung open, she jumped, and when she saw who was standing there she ran towards Taylor.

"There's my family," Oliver sneered. "You know I didn't believe it when I got a call saying you were hanging out here, being the whore to a whole biker gang, but I guess she was right."

"You need to leave," Callie said, her voice shaking. She put herself between Oliver and Taylor who had gone completely still in his seat. He'd seen far too much for his age and she hated to think what he was about to witness here. Her first instincts were to save him, she'd do anything Oliver wanted her to do, if he'd let Taylor go.

"Not leaving without what's mine," Oliver said, low and menacing. He took a step forward and in the door behind him stepped Janet and Brandon.

How the hell had they found Oliver? How did they know?

"You left this at the restaurant," Janet said with a sneer, throwing Callie's purse at her.

Shit, how had she not even noticed that it was missing? She knew the answer to that. After what happened with Mick, her mind had been on nothing else.

"Come with me Callie, and I won't have to hurt you," Oliver said.

Callie knew it was a lie, but she also knew that he'd hurt her if she didn't, all that mattered was Taylor. She needed him safe.

"Sure, but Taylor stays here, he's got friends."

"I'm not leaving my son behind with a bunch of lousy criminal bikers."

Callie motioned behind her back for Taylor to run. She heard him gasp a sob then bolt toward the back of the building.

"Where's that little asshole going?" Oliver snapped.

"You want me to go with you, fine, let's go," Callie said, stepping forward knowing she was probably walking to her own horrible death. At least Taylor would survive and if he was going to be raised by someone other than herself, she couldn't imagine anyone better than Tara and Mick. Taylor would be happy here with the pack, and she knew the pack would keep him safe from Oliver.

"Go get the boy," Oliver demanded of Janet and Callie had a moment of panic, but the woman crossed her arms over her chest and shook her head.

"No way, are you crazy? If I walk back there into their territory I'll get my head bit off. We need to move before they get wind of us."

"I'm not afraid of a bunch of backwoods motorcycle drunks," Oliver sneered, but he darted his gaze to where Brandon stood and there was caution there. Perhaps he wasn't as confident as he wanted to seem in the face of what type of men were around these parts. Oliver had always been a tough guy, always an asshole, but he'd also always used his dad's money and influence to back up that toughness. She wasn't sure he'd ever fought anyone that wasn't half his size.

"Let's go," he snapped at Callie, lunging forward and gripping her arm painfully. "I'll get Taylor later, I don't need him around for the next few days anyway," he said darkly. "I've missed my *wife.*"

Callie didn't hold back her wince of pain and shiver of fear. She saw a familiar flicker of joy light up his eyes at the sight. He was a sadistic man, and he was going to kill her.

He dragged her out of the clubhouse and shoved her into the back seat of a waiting truck. Brandon jumped into the driver's seat and Janet sat in the passenger.

Callie scooted as far from Oliver as she could. Pressed against the door she wished she was brave enough to open it and make a run for it, but to where? She'd lead them straight to Taylor or the other children perhaps. All the adults preoccupied at the edges of the property with Madeline's birth, there might be no one who could really help her.

She was on her own against Oliver, just like always.

She wasn't sure, but she thought she spotted movement in the darkness of the trees as the truck turned and took off out of the parking lot. Maybe someone had witnessed what had happened, but what would it have looked like? Would Mick believe she'd gotten in the truck and left, abandoning Taylor?

No, but what would he do even if he did know the truth? She'd rejected him.

"You know, I think you're lucky Oliver wanted you back. I was going to just have daddy send his men to kill you," Janet said with a shrug.

Callie didn't respond, just glared at the woman.

"Don't know why anyone would choose her lazy ass over your fine as fuck ass," Oliver said to Janet, making her giggle.

Callie wanted to roll her eyes at his blatant effort to make her jealous. She couldn't care less though, if he was attracted to Janet, all the better for Callie, but she wondered what Brandon thought of it all and if this was punishment for killing his alpha.

She eyed the back of Brandon's head and he seemed to be unbothered by the conversation, just staring ahead as he drove.

Maybe him and Janet weren't a love match. Did that mean she'd find an ally in him though? Probably not, he had aided in this kidnapping, and he'd been so angry at the restaurant.

The truck grew quiet as they drove on, leaving the main road and climbing high, deep into the woods along paths that she thought barely could be called a road.

MICK

Mick was the first to hold the new member of the pack, it was tradition, and he was happy to do it. It was actually one of his favorite parts of his position, welcoming each new wolf shifter life into their little part of the world. The girl came out screaming, eyes a bright yellow and Mick gave her father a smile.

"You're going to have a hard time with this one, she's got a strong wolf inside her."

"Like her mother," Lance said, kissing Madeline on the forehead.

"What's her name?" Madeline asked.

Mick held the girl to his bare chest and let their wolves communicate in a way that only happened in the first moments after birth. It was recognizing him as its alpha and together they settled on a name. "Sunny," Mick finally said, handing the infant to her mother.

"Hello, Sunny," Lance and Madeline cooed at their new daughter. The rest of their kids rushed in from outside to meet their new sister and Mick headed outside to tell the pack the good news.

When he stepped outside he knew something was wrong. First,

he smelled bear coming from the north, not the south; then he scented Janet far too fresh and near, and mixed in was something he didn't know, but it was human. Fear iced through his veins. His pack stiffened around him, and he took off at a run for the club-house. Half the pack followed him, the other half fanned out, not knowing what was wrong but knowing that they needed to check the perimeter, count the kids, and make sure everyone was safe.

By the time Mick threw the clubhouse doors open he already knew what he was going to find.

Nothing. "He came for her. Fucking Janet."

"Christ, where's Taylor?" Ryland asked, tearing through the clubhouse and back a moment later to affirm that Taylor wasn't there either.

"Follow the kid's scent, I didn't smell him up front with the others, I don't think they took him." Which set off alarm bells in Mick's head. If Oliver came for Callie but didn't take his son, that could only mean he meant to kill her.

"What are you going to do?" Tara asked.

"I'm going to get my mate," Mick snarled and headed outside.

"I'm going with you," Tara said, already putting her helmet on.

"It's Brandon," Mick pointed out. "He's helping Janet."

"Kody wouldn't approve, but he's out of town," Tara said desperately.

"I know, stay here, find Taylor and let him know that I'll save his mother."

Tara nodded and Mick jumped on his bike then sped off with three of his pack following.

CHAPTER 21

CALLIE

After about two hours of driving Oliver got impatient.

"Where the hell is this cabin at?"

"Almost there, sweet cheeks, hold yourself," Janet said.

When the truck broke through a small clearing a few minutes later, there was a small cabin. It looked like it had maybe two rooms and likely no bathroom by the looks of the little house a few yards away from it. It was seemingly in good condition though; Callie saw nice curtains hanging in the windows and a newer swing on the porch. But it was in the middle of nowhere, with absolutely no hope of finding help for whatever Oliver was about to do to her.

"Here we are!" Janet said with glee and hopped out of the truck.

Oliver frowned at the cabin as he pulled Callie out of the truck. "This looks like a dump, what the hell?"

"This is a place no one will find your little wife," Janet said with a shrug. "I held up my end of the bargain." She held out her hand.

"And I removed the threat to what you want," Oliver said, shaking Callie. "I'll pay you when I see that we weren't followed."

Janet looked ready to snap and snarl and Callie hoped she would, but then Brandon stepped close and whispered something in her ear that had her backing down.

"Fine, I'm going for a walk. I'll check the perimeter," Janet said then turned and entered the woods.

Oliver dragged Callie to the front door and opened it as if he owned the place, shoving her ahead of him, obviously assuming if there was danger, she'd take the hit and not him.

Always the gentleman, she grumbled to herself.

The place was small. One room consisted of the living, kitchen, and dining area. One door indicated a bedroom, and that was it.

"Make yourself useful and get in there, find me something to eat," Oliver demanded, shoving her toward the kitchen.

Brandon had come in behind them and prowled around, he opened the one door and Callie could see it was indeed a bedroom, decorated in bright yellows that seemed out of place in a cabin she assumed to be owned by wolf shifters.

"I'm going to the outhouse," Oliver grumbled and gave her a look that clearly implied if she tried anything stupid, she'd regret it. Then walked out the front door.

"Why are you helping them?" Callie asked Brandon as soon as Oliver was out of earshot. She had found stuff in the fridge to make sandwiches and started on the task, so familiar, making food for Oliver while terrified. "I was only defending myself and Mick when I shot Kyr, I didn't know ... I didn't know he was a person," she whispered the last still full of guilt for taking a life.

"Kyr was my friend and alpha, and I don't like Mick," Brandon said with a grunt.

"But you do like Janet?" She said with shock.

"No, but I am looking to make a deal with her father."

Callie frowned as she spread mayo on bread. That didn't sound good for Mick's pack.

"Why not make a deal with Mick?"

"He won't support my vision of the future," Brandon said ominously.

"Oh, I think he'd be happy to give you whatever you asked for if you'd leave his pack in peace, I mean, shit, he was willing to marry Janet to try and gain it."

"No, his loyalties lie elsewhere."

"Why are you so sure?"

"Because of Tara," he growled.

That shut her up and things started to slot into place. This wasn't the alpha of the bear clan, but here he was trying to make sly deals with Janet's father. He was trying to go around Kody and Kody wouldn't like it. Mick would side with Kody because Mick knew Kody would want what's best for Tara's pack.

Callie trembled with the knowledge that she really had no friends here. She was going to have to save herself if Mick didn't somehow figure out where she was in time.

Callie looked down at the meat she was placing on the bread and frowned. Was she really hoping Mick would show up and kill Oliver? She would be more than thankful, but it wasn't what she wanted, right? Death wasn't something to hope for, not even in this situation. She just wanted Oliver gone from her life.

Though the thought of him going on to hurt someone else made her stomach twist.

Maybe she did want him to die ... and what did that say about her?

She handed Brandon a sandwich and plated the others for Oliver and Janet. She couldn't eat, her stomach was twisted so tight she thought she might puke.

Oliver came back in and she handed him the sandwich she'd made. He grinned at her as if to say he'd known she'd fall right back into line. But she wouldn't. She would never again be what he wanted. Without Taylor here to keep her afraid of dying at Oliver's hands, she had nothing to stop her from fighting back.

"After I finish this, you and me are going to have a talk in the bedroom," Oliver said around a mouthful of food. He'd always had a terrible habit of talking with food in his mouth and she had lost count of the times she'd watched bits of food spray around their table while he threatened her in some manner.

His words filled her with a familiar fear but she refused to accept it.

"I don't want to be your wife anymore. I won't be your wife, Oliver."

"Oh, I think I'll change your mind soon enough," he said, anger lacing his words.

She knew she was setting him off, but she refused to go down without a fight. She'd sat and taken his abuse so long and she wouldn't, not anymore. Even if it was the last thing she did. She likely wasn't making it back to Taylor either way, so she might as well fight with her last breaths.

Brandon looked from her to Oliver and raised one eyebrow, as if he couldn't wait to see how this played out. He and Janet would be glad to get rid of her. Would Janet continue to align herself with Brandon? Would she manage to form some kind of takeover of the bear clan from Kody? Or would she slink back to Mick with some kind of deal from her daddy?

The thought of that mangy woman in Mick's bed filled her with jealous rage and she was so distracted she didn't realize Oliver was talking to her until she felt the sting of his hit on her cheek.

"I said I'm done, take the fucking plate and wash it," he seethed.

Callie held a cool hand to her now burning cheek, tears in her eyes from the pain but she refused to cry. He'd never been moved by her tears, she'd learned that first; her tears only made him happier with what he was doing, so she tried to never give him any.

"And I said I am not your wife anymore," Callie said, dropping her hand and readying herself for a blow that would likely send her to the ground, bleeding.

He did lash out, but he didn't strike, instead he grabbed her by the hair and shoved her toward the bedroom.

"We'll be right back," he said to Brandon.

But Callie wasn't going in there with him easily. She twisted and pushed at his body. He was surprised by her resistance, something she'd never done. She put her hands on him to fight, to get away. He wasn't prepared and she was able to get free, she sprinted for the front door.

It opened and there stood Janet, just slipping her shirt back on, apparently having gone wolf to walk the perimeter.

"What the fuck," Janet said as Callie slammed into her.

"I'm not his wife and I refuse to be treated like his slave and punching bag," she snarled.

"Look, honey, I don't blame ya. He ain't no Mick, but he's the one who's taking you out of my way." Janet said and held her arm tight, preventing her from leaving.

Brandon watched it all from his seat on the couch.

"What the hell is that supposed to mean?" Oliver snapped at Janet.

"It means you're as worthless as her, except in the way you can get her out of here and the cash you're going to give me for the trouble."

Oliver was too angry to take lip from any woman apparently because he pulled back and punched Janet in the mouth. "You won't get shit from me, bitch."

"Hey now," Brandon growled as Janet howled in pain. "She's not yours to do with as you please."

"I don't give a fuck. No one stands between me and what's mine, not even you, asshole. You're just the muscle, remember that or I won't be giving you a payment either."

Callie saw the rage spark in Brandon's eyes and wondered if Oliver had any idea what they were; she doubted it because he looked shocked when Janet didn't collapse with his punch. She was bleeding though and breathing hard, looking pissed off and about to shift, Callie would guess by the yellow of her eyes. Which may or may not be a good thing. Janet didn't like her, but she also didn't like Oliver at this point, who would Janet attack if she lost it?

"I'm the one saying no, Oliver," Callie snapped at him to get his attention off Janet and hopefully give the woman a moment to calm down.

He turned to her and sneered. "And I know how to take care of that." He grabbed her hair and pulled her behind him toward the bedroom. Callie struggled but he was expecting it this time and only paused long enough to shake her violently, making her head spin and her eyes fuzz, then he started dragging her along again. She gripped his hands to try and relieve some of the pressure, but it didn't do anything other than rip open the healing burn wounds on her hand.

She was desperate, she looked back at Janet, still standing by the door looking pissed but her eyes were no longer yellow.

"If you help me, I swear I'll leave. I'll take Taylor and I'll leave Mick to you," Callie begged, desperate to live, to do what she'd started out to do so long ago. Get away somewhere safe with Taylor.

"Won't matter if his wolf has claimed you already," she snarled.

"It hasn't."

"Shut up, bitch," Oliver said opening the bedroom door. "You're mine and no one is here to help you."

"Please, I told him no, Janet, I swear, I turned Mick down."

Janet's eyes widened.

"I said shut up!" Oliver snapped and pushed her into the room. Callie stumbled and fell, hitting her head against a table. She saw stars and crumpled, trying to will away the pain, to hold on to her consciousness and her fight instincts. She stumbled to her feet as the door slammed and Oliver laughed.

Growling and crashing erupted in the other room, but Oliver wasn't swayed from his pursuit. He stalked toward her, and the bedroom door exploded behind him. A black wolf jumped through the door and onto Oliver's back, its jaws wrapping around Oliver's neck.

Oliver was dead almost instantly, blood spraying all over Callie and the room.

Callie shivered, frozen in fear, staring up into the familiar wolf face of Mick.

He shifted and crouched in front of her, completely nude. Callie was too shocked to appreciate his form however, and just stared dumbly at his face.

"Callie? Are you okay?" he asked softly.

"I—I don't know," she said with a shaky laugh.

"Did he hurt you?" he asked with gritted teeth.

"Not much."

"Any is not okay," he said, eyes flashing yellow.

"What did you do?" she asked, suddenly remembering there were two other people in this cabin, had he killed them too?

Mick frowned and leaned back. "He was hurting you. He kidnapped you. Callie, you know that he wasn't going to give up and go away, this had to be done."

"Oh," she said, looking down at the body of her once husband. She *was* glad he was dead, and she'd probably process the whole ordeal when she calmed down.

"Can I take you home, I'm sure Taylor is worried, Ryland was looking for him when I left, I think he's hiding."

"I told him to run, I didn't want him to see whatever Oliver was going to do. I didn't want Oliver to take him too."

"That's good, that was the right thing, I'm sure he's fine, let's go to him."

"I knew he'd be safe with the pack."

"Always," Mick agreed. "Can I help you up?"

Callie nodded and relief filled Mick's features. He helped her to stand, and she tried not to look at herself but she could feel the blood sticky on her face and neck. "I need this off of me," she said, suddenly desperate. "Mick I need his blood off of me," she was yelling now, panic and relief and fear all mixed in and rushing over her.

"Okay, okay, Callie, calm down. I need you to trust me. I am going to help you clean up a bit, and when we get home, you can shower. We can't stay here longer than necessary though. We are deep in Royal's territory."

She nodded, her head feeling heavy and her neck unhinged. He reached up and stopped her head from continuing its movement, then grabbed a clean blanket and used it to wipe her face, chest and arms as best he could.

"Better?" he asked.

She nodded but it was a lie, she felt just as disgusting. Because she was glad, so very glad that Oliver's blood was spattered across the room.

Mick led her out of the bedroom. The living space was a mess, splintered front door, broken furniture, splatters of blood, but no bodies.

"Where's Janet and Brandon?" Callie asked.

"They both ran as soon as I came in. I think Brad went after them. He sunk his teeth into Janet's leg and Brandon smacked at him. They tussled as I went through the bedroom door." He swallowed and his eyes flashed yellow. "I could smell your fear, Callie, and I was terrified I was going to walk into something I couldn't save you from. I didn't know if I was too late."

Callie stopped on the porch and turned to face him. "Thank you," she said. "Thank you for coming after me, even after—after everything." She looked away, guilty for how she'd rejected him.

"I had no choice, Callie. I know you don't understand but there is nothing that would keep me from saving you."

"Because your wolf wants me," she said, looking away and noticing for the first time that they weren't alone. Three other pack members were pulling on clothing near their bikes and trying to not be obvious about watching them with yellow eyes.

"He would do anything to protect you, he's decided you're it for him, Callie."

"And it doesn't matter what you want?"

Confusion flashed through Mick's eyes. "I am the wolf, Callie. We are separate but not. I want you in a human way, and he wants you in a soul entwining, never-ending sort of way."

"You're right, I don't understand," she said with a shake of her head. "But it doesn't matter right now, does it? We should get out of here."

CHAPTER 22

KODY

Kody was exhausted as he pulled up in front of his trailer. He'd had to get Ava out, and there'd been no time to waste. He hated that it meant he'd cancelled the coffee date with Tara but he knew she'd understand when he explained fully.

He pulled his phone out and texted her as he walked to his porch, hoping she'd agree to have that coffee tomorrow. He had a lot to explain actually.

The smell of wolf had him freezing, one hand on the door-knob. He turned slowly, his instincts to shift already making his skin tight.

"Royal," Kody acknowledged the wolf but his gaze darted to the three bear shifters standing close behind him. Not the elders, these were men who had been very dedicated to Kyr, no doubt some of the men who would have continued to use Ava if he hadn't gotten her safely away.

He'd known he was going to have to deal with them, but he hadn't expected to face an alpha wolf as well.

"My daughter has gotten in her head that she'll have one of you and I'm here to make sure she gets the alpha."

Kody laughed, this was ridiculous, but at least it wasn't an attack. "Well, your daughter is something, but I'm not interested in marrying her. I have a mate and she's in a different pack old man, sorry."

"It's not you I want anymore," Janet said, stepping out of the woods, Brandon at her side. They both looked like they'd been in a fight but came out of it fine, unfortunately. Janet ran a hand up and down Brandon's arm and gazed up at him with pouty lips and wide eyes. "Brandon is strong and capable. I'm taking him, but he needs to be alpha, or daddy won't agree."

Royal nodded as if the words his daughter spoke made perfect sense.

Kody looked with wide, shocked eyes at the gathered clan members who seemed to be supporting this insanity. "What the fuck is this?"

"You wouldn't even avenge your brother's murder," Shane spat from behind Royal.

"You think you can just come along and start changing the way things are done?" Jerry growled. "Brandon will bring Ava back."

Kody looked at Brandon and realized what was happening; a mutiny, a challenge for his position, and there was nothing he could do but answer it.

Laura ran around the corner and took in the scene with fear in her eyes.

"Get the elders," he snarled at her, "Brandon wants to challenge me."

Kody was going to make sure this went down fair, it was him and Brandon, the others would have to stay back unless they wanted to challenge him after. Kody hoped not, he wasn't sure he'd have the strength. He hadn't slept in two days and fighting Brandon was likely to take everything else out of him.

Laura returned with the elders and quickly the rest of the clan followed. There were no clear sides as everyone circled Kody and Brandon. They were one clan, they could have only one leader and they would all respect the results of this fight.

Brandon and Kody stripped and circled each other then when the elders gave the signal, they shifted to attack. This was part of the battle, because an alpha should be able to shift the fastest, he should be able to pull on the support of the pack. If Kody didn't have the support of the pack and Brandon did, then he'd shift faster and he'd attack while Kody was most vulnerable.

Kody felt the bear flow through his body, he felt his senses change to the bear and he roared as he leapt at Brandon a split second before Brandon's own change was complete. It wasn't much, but it was enough for Kody to feel confident in his clan. They were behind him.

The sounds of their clashing, roaring, and crashing drifted north.

TARA

Tara let Taylor out of her arms when Callie jumped off of Mick's bike. The two embraced with tears and Mick watched with joy and grief. Tara felt for her brother, he looked so unsure of what would happen next.

She felt her phone buzz and saw a text from Kody, he was back and wanted to get coffee in the morning. She didn't want to wait that long. After what she'd seen today, she needed to talk to Kody. She sent him a text to meet her now and headed for the border.

He didn't respond but when she got close to the border she heard the sounds of a fight and she froze, she checked her phone again, nothing. Fear spiked and she ran straight into bear clan territory, no thoughts of her own safety, she had to know Kody was okay.

When she saw the circle of bear clan members she had no doubt as to what was happening. This was an alpha battle, and that meant Kody was in there fighting for his life.

She gasped and covered her mouth so she wouldn't scream for him like she wanted, wouldn't distract him. She heard a terrible wet ripping, and the circle froze. Tara couldn't hold back, she had to know.

"Kody!" she screamed and ran forward, the circle opened for her and she saw two bloody men lying in the dirt. It brought back memories of that day, when it had been her blood and Allen's, and panic nearly choked her. But this wasn't her blood, this wasn't a human torn to pieces for hurting her, this was the world they lived in, the rules they lived by. And this could be the death of her mate. "Kody," she sobbed, dropping to her knees. Were they both dead? Everyone was so still, not even a bird chirped as they waited.

Then there was movement, and Kody stood, naked, bloody, and victorious. His eyes locked onto her and he stalked forward. Tara looked up at him from her knees, tears in her eyes unable to speak.

He was alive.

"Tara," he snarled, chest heaving, muscles bulging.

"You bitch!" Janet's voice shocked Tara and she didn't react fast enough. Janet knocked her over and clawed at her face and pulled at her hair.

Tara focused quickly and got the upper hand, twisting until she was on top of Janet and punched her twice in the face before she was yanked off of the now cowering woman.

Tara wriggled and yanked against the arms until she heard Kody's soothing voice. "Leave her, she isn't worth the effort."

Tara turned in his arms and wrapped her arms around his neck, pulling him down for a deep kiss. She tasted blood on his lips and it excited her wolf. She jumped and wrapped her legs around Kody's waist, desperate for more.

Kody's hands gripped her ass and held her tight as his tongue swept through her mouth, laying claim to her.

By the time he pulled away Tara was panting, her wolf was howling, and she could think of nothing other than having this man, this bear.

"I am alpha here; I have proven it and I will take on any other challengers," Kody announced.

"No," Tara whispered but she understood, this is what he had to do even if it terrified her.

No one spoke up. Still clasping Tara to him he spun around slowly and waited. Tara saw the clan look down, look away and she saw Royal dragging his daughter toward his truck. Janet was eyeing them with rage, her eyes yellow with her wolf.

"Then know this, my clan. Tara, wolf shifter, is my mate. For me there will be no other and any who think to harm her or challenge our bond will meet with a swift and fierce punishment."

Tara shivered at his words. He paused again for any arguments that might come but when none did, he looked at her, his eyes bright with his bear.

"Tara, will you be mine?" he asked. She could see the worry in his features, he still wasn't sure she'd accept him.

"Yes," she whispered and the rumble in his chest matched her own, their animals rejoicing.

"You idiot!" Janet screamed, breaking from her father and running back toward them. "He is the reason you were attacked. He is the one who pushed Allen to the edge that morning, meeting him and telling him how he was coming for you! Then he showed up at your restaurant and made sure the asshole fell over that edge. He's the reason Allen didn't hold back. Kody pushed him to nearly kill you then swooped in and saved the day." Janet sneered as she dropped that bomb.

Royal grabbed her and threw her over his shoulder and hauled her away in the remaining silence.

Tara pulled away from Kody and saw the truth of Janet's words on his face. "Kody?"

"I didn't know he'd hurt you like that, Tara. I would never do anything to harm you, never do anything to put you in harm's way, you have to know that. I didn't know he was like that, I just thought I could talk to him man to man and let him know my intentions, maybe scare him off."

Tara reached up and touched his face, she saw the fear in his eyes, the anguish and truth. She stretched her body up and pulled him down, kissing him softly. "I forgive you," she whispered against his lips.

Kody growled and pulled her up into his arms again then walked her to his trailer, storming through the door and straight to the bedroom. He dropped her on the bed and towered over her, bloody and yearning.

"Do you want me to shower before I claim you?" he asked, his voice strained

Tara licked her lips and looked at all of him without an ounce of shame. "Quickly," she ordered.

He growled, disappointed in her answer then turned and leaped to the bathroom. The water turned on and while Tara listened to the sounds of him washing she stripped out of her clothes and tried to calm her nerves. She knew he wasn't going to hurt her, but was she ready for him to possess her?

When he walked back into the bedroom his hair was wet and he had a towel wrapped around his waist. He dropped it as soon as he saw she was naked.

"I was afraid you were going to change your mind," he admitted.

"I think I've fought it long enough, Kody, you're my mate."

"I'm your mate," he agreed.

He kissed her and laid her back on the bed, his body covering hers. He was so big, and it thrilled her. She'd dreamed about this moment and yet she couldn't have imagined the feeling of completeness that being this close and intimate with him would bring. She ran her hands up and down his back as he devoured her mouth. His hands slipped down and under her ass and around her thighs then pulled them apart. She wiggled against his hard cock, eager.

He growled and broke the kiss, trailing his lips across her cheek to her ear. "When I take you, I am going to bite you here," he licked her neck. "Solidifying our bond."

"I understand," she panted. "Please, Kody I don't want to wait any longer."

He rumbled with satisfied laughter and nipped at her lobe then kissed his way down her body. She growled in frustration, her hands in his hair, tugging, she wanted him, all of him, now.

"I am in control," he growled against her belly and continued south as she trembled with desire.

His mouth landed on her curls and she forgot all arguments as his tongue swept over her engorged clit.

"Fuck, Kody, yes!" she screamed, her body convulsing already. It had been so long, and she wasn't going to be able to hold back. His fingers moved gently over her slit and entered her, his teeth scraped her clit and she was done in three strokes. She came with a wildness she'd never experienced before, her body curling and bowing, her thighs trapping him as her hands tugged on his hair.

And all the while he continued to lick, nip and suck, to thrust and take her as far as possible on those waves of pleasure.

When she was mewling with satisfaction, limp and desperate for more, he raised up and looked at her with deep satisfaction. "I could live the rest of my life between your thighs, Tara. I could eat only you and die happy."

"Fuck me," she demanded.

He laughed and kissed her, lining up his cock. "Mine," he growled against her lips as he thrust forward. His strokes were controlled, long and smooth as he drove her wild again. He kissed her lips, her neck, her ear. His hands were on her breasts, pinching her nipples and then he was holding her hips and thrusting harder, losing his control and she loved it. Her nails scratched down his back and pressed into his ass, begging for more, she wanted everything he could give her.

With a roar he pulled out, flipped her over and shoved her face down, ass up. He entered her again, one hand on her shoulder, one on her hip he directed their movements to his satisfaction. Tara clung to the pillow under her and gasped her pleasure into it. She could feel another orgasm so close and something more. Something she'd never experienced before.

Her wolf, right there under the surface was rippling with anticipation.

"Kody," she begged, sure that she needed him to bite her, knowing that's what her body was asking for, what her wolf was waiting for.

Kody seemed to understand. He leaned over her, his mouth on the space between her neck and shoulder, he licked her and continued his thrusting then she felt his teeth and she was lost. A prick of pain and then a roar of pleasure. His hips stuttered, her orgasm exploded, and the mate bond clicked into place, completing her.

She cried and collapsed. Kody held her trembling body, neither speaking while they felt the new awareness of each other, their animals speaking to each other and reveling in the bond that had been created.

"I had no idea it could be this good," Tara admitted.

"I knew it would be, with you it could be nothing else."

Chapter 23

Mick

Mick watched Callie walk away with Taylor wrapped in her arms. That was his family walking away and it hurt to watch. He wanted to be a part of the comfort and reunion. He wanted to wrap them both in his arms and vow to keep them safe always.

He turned to Brad. "Keep a watch, I want to know if Janet gets within a hundred yards of our territory and I expect to see her father before night falls tomorrow."

"Will do," Brad said.

Mick made his way to Tara's cabin, unable to help himself. The whole ride back all he could think about was that Callie didn't need him now. She was safe from her husband, and her car was fixed. She could leave at any time, she could go back to her home, her life.

She could leave him.

Tara's cabin door opened when he approached. Taylor stood there staring at him.

"How's it going?" he asked because he didn't know what else to say to the boy who he'd started to think of as his own.

"Mom's in the shower."

He nodded. "She's okay, I made sure she was okay and you too, Taylor. You are both safe now."

Taylor nodded and looked at his feet. "Are we going to leave now? Now that my dad's really gone?" There was a sadness to his voice that broke Mick's heart.

"I don't know, Taylor. It's complicated and it's for the adults to worry about, not you, you just get to be a kid and have fun."

"I have fun here."

"I know."

Taylor nodded and went back inside. Mick couldn't bring himself to leave so he sat on the steps and waited.

Half an hour later the door opened again and the wind brought him the citrus scent of his mate. She sat down beside him cautiously. Her arms were wrapped around herself and the bruises on her face were visible in the moon's light. He wanted to rip that man apart again and he lifted his lip in a snarl.

"I'm sorry I've brought such trouble to your pack," she finally said, looking down at the ground.

He reached over and took her unburned hand. She was trembling and cold, he wanted to wrap her in his arms, in his bed, and never let her go. But he had to get through to her, and that meant he had to be honest in a way that scared the shit out of him.

The thought of her leaving and taking Taylor broke him, he knew he'd never survive it.

"Callie, I need to tell you something that just might change everything for us. But I want to make sure you're ready to hear it. If your mind is too full, if your body is still too filled with the fear and chaos of what happened earlier, then we can talk in the morning. You can go back inside and sleep safe knowing that I'm out here watching."

"I think Taylor and I should leave," she whispered.

He glared at her words, he'd expected them, but they still made him angry, and his wolf frightened. "Where would you rather be than here?" he demanded, squeezing her hands for emphasis.

"I don't know, I guess ... with Oliver gone, we should go back home."

"To what? You didn't have a job, you didn't have friends, and Taylor has never been happier, you said it yourself."

Callie looked away. "I just, I just don't know that this is the best place for us."

"Because you're afraid of me?" He didn't want to hear her answer.

"Yes, but not for the reason you think."

"Callie, look at me. Let me ease whatever weighs on your mind."

She met his gaze again, her eyes wet with unshed tears. "I'm afraid I'm not strong enough to keep you from taking over my life," she admitted. "I'm afraid I will be crushed under the weight of your dominance. I'm afraid that I still won't know who I am if I stay here. I never had the opportunity to find myself. I think it's something I'm missing to make me whole."

Those words blew him away. They were so real and raw, and he could see them reflected in her eyes. She wanted to be her own person, and his wolf wanted to own every part of her existence. She wasn't wrong. It wasn't about her fear of his wolf or her fear of being harmed. She was afraid of never finding herself.

He couldn't take that from her, she deserved everything, that was one thing he and his wolf agreed on. His wolf just didn't agree with how to give it to her.

Mick dropped her hand and stood, holding his wolf tighter than he'd ever had to hold him before.

"You're right. You should go. You deserve to find out who you are without anyone else."

She looked shocked by his agreement and a little hurt he thought too, but that might just be wishful thinking. He had to walk away before he changed his mind and tried to force her to stay.

It was the hardest thing he'd ever had to do in his life.

CALLIE

Callie hurried inside before she could throw herself at him. There was a desperation inside of her that wanted to do what was easy. To become whatever he wanted her to be.

But if she did that, she'd always wonder if she truly had ever known herself.

The next morning she had everything packed, it was easy, there wasn't much that was theirs. Taylor moped and was out saying goodbye to all the kids. Tara met her in the living room with a sad look on her face.

"You're breaking his heart," Tara said.

"I think mine too," Callie said with a sob.

Tara crossed to her and wrapped her arms around Callie. "He'll be waiting for you, whenever you want to come back," she whispered.

"And if I don't?"

"Then he'll still wait, that's what the whole wolf's mate thing does. I know it sounds ridiculous and scary, but I promise you it's not."

Callie pulled back and wiped her eyes. "Wow, way to guilt a girl."

"Truth, I figured you should know. That way if and when you decide you've figured yourself out, you know he's ready and waiting. He won't be with someone else."

Callie pushed the guilt away as she walked outside to call Taylor. Madeline was there with the new baby and so many others she'd come to know and call friends. She gave them all waves but she couldn't talk, it was too hard and Mick was noticeably absent.

Lance took her bags and walked her to the car. "It's in great condition, should run forever."

Callie threw her arms around the man and sobbed. "Thank you, for everything."

He just grunted and pulled away. "Mick's a good man," he said and turned and walked away, leaving her with more guilt, more confusion.

"Do we really have to go?" Taylor asked.

"Yeah, we really do," Callie said but she wasn't confident, and she stared at the clubhouse for a minute, wondering if it had been fate that brought her here and if she was denying its wisdom by leaving now.

———

"We're home," Callie said five days later as they pulled up in front of the familiar garage. She had more money left in her purse than she'd had the last time she sat in this driveway, and she was free of her abusive husband with no fear of him tracking her down.

She should be ecstatic for her future.

So why did she feel overwhelmed by dread and as if she'd left the best possibility for her and Taylor's future behind?

"I miss the pack," Taylor said sullenly.

He'd reiterated the sentiment at least three times a day since they'd left. She didn't even know what to say to comfort him.

"Things will be different here now," she promised him. But he didn't respond and neither of them moved to get out of the car despite the long hours they'd driven the last few days.

Callie turned around to look at her pouting son and gave him as convincing a smile as she could muster around her own confusing feelings.

"How about we order pizza and watch a movie?"

His eyes lit up, "Okay, but I want all cheese."

"Deal," she said.

Callie wasn't prepared for the feeling of walking back into that house. She took one step inside and couldn't breathe, her head swam, and she leaned against the doorjamb as every hit, every push and every word she'd suffered from Oliver ran through her mind in a horrifying slideshow.

"Actually, I want sausage," Taylor called from the living room, pulling Callie back to the present.

Callie ordered the pizza and walked slowly through the house. She wanted to erase everything that reminded her of Oliver, but she knew she needed to be careful, she needed to act slowly. He'd be a missing person, maybe forever. It wasn't as if anyone could know that he'd been torn apart by a wolf shifter. She'd never be able to collect life insurance or access his personal bank account. Her name wasn't even on this house. He'd kept everything from her, and she had no idea what that was going to mean for her and Taylor's future here.

Had she made a terrible mistake?

That night she slept in the guest room, unable to bring herself to get into the bed where she'd been violated so many times. She went to sleep thinking of Mick, hoping he was alright and wishing she could talk to Tara and Madeline, hold the new baby, and watch Taylor play with all the kids. She wished she could look out the bedroom window and see a huge black wolf standing guard.

CHAPTER 24

MICK

Mick sat at the bar and slammed back another shot. He'd lost count of how many, and he signaled Tara for another.

"I think you should go home, Mick," Tara said, putting one hand on her hip and giving him a sympathetic look that annoyed him because it was all he'd seen from everyone in the pack for the last four days since Callie and Taylor had left.

"My home left me," he snarled.

"The way I see it, you have two choices. Go get her, or shut up. You can't drink yourself into an oblivion every day, we need a pack alpha."

Tara's words stung because he knew she was speaking of the way their father had been.

"Another," Mick demanded.

Tara poured him a shot and frowned at him as he picked it up, staring down into the amber liquid.

"That's not going to replace her and it's not going to give you the courage to do what needs to be done."

"And what's that, sister?"

"You need to tell her what it means to be a wolf shifter mate. You need to trust her enough to not abuse that power."

Mick hated that she was right.

"I had to trust Kody; you know how hard that was."

Mick grunted. He had never seen his sister happier than she'd been since mating with the bear. He had to admit it was irritating. He was suffering and a part of him wished everyone else around him was suffering too. But they weren't. Everywhere he looked he saw happily mated couples and it just made his loss sharper.

He left the shot on the bar and walked out of the clubhouse. He froze halfway to his cabin and turned, heading for his bike.

He didn't know if Callie would ever accept him and what his wolf wanted from her, but he knew that he couldn't not try. He didn't want to deny what would make them both complete and the only way he could avoid a life of desperation and depression was if he trusted Callie the way he was asking her to trust him.

CALLIE

Callie woke up with a plan. She made coffee and pulled up the want ads. She made Taylor breakfast and found exactly two jobs she was qualified for, maid and waitress. Neither had good hours or good pay and she wasn't sure what she was supposed to do without access to Oliver's money to pay the house payment and other bills likely due in the next week. But it was a step in the right direction.

Not to mention there was a police report she should be filing.

A missing person's report?

How was she supposed to explain any of the last month to the police? Maybe she should just take what she could out of the house and run. But then she was back to barely better off than when she left Oliver with nothing to start over with, and Taylor didn't deserve to live that kind of life.

Callie looked at Taylor, sitting alone and staring outside with a sour expression on his face. Everything she did from here needed to be what was best for him.

"Do you want to go out and play after breakfast?"

"With who? There aren't any kids my age close by."

"That's not true, the Stevenson twins are right across the street."

"Yeah, and they hate me. They think I'm weird and told the whole school I eat my boogers."

Callie's mom heart hurt and her protective instincts bristled. She wanted to march across the street and have a conversation with Mrs. Stevenson, but she knew it wouldn't help. Kids did that sort of thing all the time and unfortunately, it was something best left to them to sort out amongst themselves. She looked at Taylor and sighed. "We both need a fresh start, don't we?"

He shrugged and put an overflowing spoonful of cheerios into his mouth.

She spent the day looking through all the papers Oliver had stuffed in his desk and came up with nothing useful. He had everything in his name alone and unless he turned up dead, she couldn't even claim any rights as his widow.

"The asshole is dead and still screwing my life up," she grumbled as she sat on the office floor surrounded by useless papers. She had a sudden urge to burn it all; to watch this life he'd forced her into turn to ashes. So seemingly perfect and yet it had been hell.

She couldn't, she knew that, but damn she wanted to. Instead she called on the two jobs that she might be qualified for.

She had to do something, or she'd never be able to take care of Taylor.

Two days later she was home from her first day at work with a pocket full of tips and a feeling that she could do this.

She was met in the driveway by Oliver's boss and a police officer. Fear tightened her chest. She counted three deep breaths as she gathered her purse and jacket then got out of the car.

"Hey, Mr. Pilson, what can I do for you?"

"You can tell me where the hell Oliver is. That good for nothing hasn't shown up for work in over a week."

Callie had tried to prepare for this sort of situation, had

rehearsed it in front of a mirror even. "Well, I kicked him out," she said with a shrug. "I got tired of his drinking and his abuse," she didn't have to fake the wobble in her lip or tone as she said that word. It helped that she still had a bit of bruising on her face from her last interaction with Oliver. "I kicked him out and I haven't seen him since. I didn't know he wasn't going to work. I guess that means he won't be paying child support any time soon."

"You're divorcing him?" the police officer asked.

"That's the plan. I just got a job so I can save up for a lawyer."

"I'm taking it as a missing person at this point if neither of you have seen or heard from him in the last week," the officer said. "Which means that if he shows up here, or at work," he said to Mr. Pilson. "We'll need to hear about it right away."

"What if he just stays gone?" she asked then kicked herself as the officer raised his eyebrow at her. She bit her lip; she probably shouldn't have asked that.

"Then after three years you can go to court and have him declared dead, become a widow and inherit whatever he had unless there's a will of some sort claiming it goes elsewhere."

"Do I have to wait that long for a divorce?"

"No, there's a process for that sort of thing, publication in the newspaper of intent to divorce. You'll want to talk to a lawyer if you plan to go that route."

Callie nodded and the officer walked away. She was left with Mr. Pilson.

"I can't say I miss the asshole," Mr. Pilson said. "I'm going to clear out his office, if he shows up at this point, he's fired anyway. You can come pick it up or I can toss it all."

"Toss it," she said, she had no interest in Oliver's things.

Mr. Pilson nodded and walked away.

Callie walked into the house and paid the neighbor girl she'd hired to watch Taylor for the day. There went all her tips.

"Did you have a good day?" she asked Taylor as they cuddled together on the couch, a cartoon playing quietly on the television.

"It was okay, Serenity isn't very much fun, she did play cards with me though."

"Well, she's a teenage girl, Taylor, I don't think she's going to be a playmate, she's mostly here to make sure you don't burn the house down."

"Yeah, I know," he said. He'd been so sullen since they'd gotten back and she wasn't sure what to do about it. She hoped when school started and he was back with friends ... but did he even have any friends there? He'd been so happy with the pack. She'd been happy too.

As she made dinner she ran through the viability of the plan she'd come up with. Work at the diner, pay a babysitter, hire a lawyer to get a divorce ... or just wait the three years and declare him dead? Somehow pay the house payment and the other bills. Could she have a yard sale? Make some money off of Oliver's crap?

No matter what, she came up short in her mind, every time. She just wanted to walk away from it all, and there was only one place she wanted to go.

But was it too late, would Mick even want her back after she'd left him? Was she still too scared to take what he offered if he did want her back?

The rumble of an engine made her catch her breath. Moments later a strong knock at the door had her running and when she tore it open, she gasped. "Mick."

"I need to tell you everything before you make any kind of decision to stay away from me," he said quickly.

She nodded, unable to speak. It was as if her thoughts had conjured him and now here he was and all she wanted to do was throw herself into his arms and have him carry her to bed.

"Mick!" Taylor screamed and threw himself into Mick's arms the way Callie wanted to. "You're here."

"I'm here," Mick agreed. "I need to talk to your mom; do you think you could give us a few minutes alone?"

"Sure, I'll go out in the back yard but after, will you play catch with me?"

"Of course," Mick said and set the boy down.

Taylor smiled wide at Callie, a bigger smile than she'd seen in days and ran off out the back door.

"Come in, do you want something to drink?" Callie asked, leading him to the kitchen. "I was just making dinner. Are you hungry?"

"I'd love a glass of water," he said with a gruff voice that sent a shiver down her spine.

He followed her closely and the scent and heat of his body was like a caress she wanted to lean into, but she didn't. He'd come to talk, and she needed to listen. She handed him the water and they both sat at the small dining table.

"My wolf claimed you as his the moment you stepped into the clubhouse. He scented you and said you're his, *ours*. I know that sounds scary and weird and domineering even, but there's another part of it that you need to know."

She couldn't answer, she just nodded.

"My wolf would never harm you, but it's more than that, too. A wolf gives up his will to its mate in a way that is so complete you could tell him to sit and stay and he wouldn't move for the rest of his life if you didn't come back and say get up. He would wither and die before breaking your commands."

"That sounds horrible," she admitted. She had never wanted that kind of control over someone.

"It can be," he agreed. "But it can also be beautiful and perfect. I've seen it both ways. Look at Lance and Madeline, they are so perfectly mated, and they would never use that power to harm the other. But my parents," he paused, his voice cracking and he shook his head. "My parents had problems. Neither of them were very good at being faithful or kind, and they both drank too much. One night my father came home after carousing; he was the alpha of the pack and at times he used that power to sleep with other females. My mom had been drinking and she got mad enough that night to send him out to the frozen lake and jump in. He never came back up and when she realized what she'd done, she took her own life. She couldn't live with the guilt I guess. Tara and I weren't enough for her to live for. You see, the wolf might choose its perfect mate, but that doesn't guarantee the human parts will align too. My mother was human, like you, and she struggled with the pack life but it's because of the way my father ran the pack. I am not my father, and you are not my mother, and I have to realize that I can trust you if I am asking you to trust me." He stopped then and stared into Callie's eyes. "I want you as much as my wolf, but I was afraid of what it would mean to accept a mate. I think that's why I was so willing to marry Janet. It was more than just about gaining the help of her father. It would keep me safe from the kind of power a mate has over me. But Callie, I don't regret finding you. I just needed the time to realize that you're perfect for me because I can trust you to never abuse your power over me. Do you trust me, Callie, to take care of you and Taylor?"

Callie was frozen, stuck in his gaze and the memories he'd shared with her. It was horrifying and she wanted to cradle him in her arms and tell him that he was safe with her. But she needed to figure out if she believed the same. Was she safe with him? Did she believe that down to her soul?

"I do," she whispered.

Mick howled and lifted her up, embracing her. His mouth was hot on hers and she moaned as she accepted him.

Callie pulled back before things could get out of hand. "Can I make you dinner?" she asked.

He growled but let her go, his eyes yellow. "You can make me anything you want, but tonight, I'm going to make you mine." His words were a low growl, and she felt her panties soak as the sound vibrated through her.

"Deal," she whispered.

MICK

That night after Mick read Taylor a bedtime story and tucked the kid into bed he found Callie standing in the dark kitchen staring out at the yard. She had her arms wrapped around her body and she was so deep in thought she didn't even seem to hear him approach.

He took a moment to admire her. She was wearing a pair of leggings with an oversized T-shirt and fuzzy socks on her feet. Her hair was pulled up in a bun with tendrils falling down her neck. She was beautiful and he couldn't believe he was about to make her his.

Ours, his wolf growled through his head.

She spun around as if she'd heard the word too, her eyes wide.

"Hey princess, I think he's asleep."

"It's weird for me, to let you do something like that, a fatherly thing. His own father never even did that. Couldn't be bothered."

He wanted to kill the asshole all over again for the way he'd made these two wonderful people suffer.

"I am prepared to be everything for you and Taylor." He ran a finger along her jawline. "Are you prepared to be everything for me and my wolf?"

"Yes," she said as her body trembled under his touch.

"Take me to a bedroom or I'm going to fuck you on the table," he growled.

She took his hand and he let her lead him to a room that he had a feeling wasn't the one she'd shared with Oliver, it was far too sparsely decorated and there was no sign of a masculine influence.

Mick shut the door behind him, and she turned to face him. "What's it like?" she asked, and he knew she meant the mate mark he wanted to give her and not the sex, she'd experienced a bit of that with him already and had seemed to enjoy it very much.

"I will bring you to the height of pleasure," he promised. "Then I will bite you, here." He touched the space where her neck and shoulder met.

"Will it hurt?" She was breathing heavily, her voice a whisper, and he could smell her arousal.

The reassurance that she was all in pleased his wolf deeply and he knew his eyes had to be mostly yellow as he stared into hers. "It will be a sharp pain I'm told, but it won't hurt long before the mate link is set, and the pleasure will be exquisite."

"But I'm not like you. Is it the same, even if I'm human?"

"It is." God he hoped he was right, but it's not like he could ask his mother.

"Okay," Callie said and grabbed his face. "I am sure it will be perfect."

He appreciated her confidence and hoped she'd keep it through to the end. Before she could think about it any more he started to kiss her softly. All along her jaw and to her ear. He nipped at her lobe and down her neck. She trembled and her hands grasped his shoulders.

His wolf was impatient, but he held it back, stepping away far enough to lift her shirt over her head. She wasn't wearing a bra, and his mouth was drawn to her nipples, pink and pert. He pulled first one and then the other into his mouth. Her hands gripped his hair and she moaned. He was gripping her hips, his thumbs massaging circles on her abdomen, teasing her with how close he was to where he knew she needed him.

"Mick," she groaned, her hands pushing desperately on him.

He obliged, kissing down her belly as his hands peeled her leggings down. He dove in between her legs, his tongue seeking out her sweet center. "I haven't been able to get this taste out of my mind since that night."

"Oh, Mick."

He growled and lapped at her, pulling one of her legs over his shoulder and he didn't let up until she was gushing on his tongue.

He stood and kissed her mouth deeply then led her to the bed as he shed his own clothes.

"Are you ready for me?"

She nodded eagerly and spread her legs, offering herself to him with the most delicious display of her body. He slid between her legs and kissed her until she was writhing and arching. Then, when he knew she was ready, he slipped inside of her and the feeling of being one with his mate overwhelmed him. It was unlike anything he'd ever experienced in his life. Her body fit him perfectly and made him want to stay there forever. As he slid in and out, he watched her face for any sign of discontent, any hint of regret or second thoughts. It would quite possibly kill him, but he would stop if she changed her mind. He would never do anything to cause her pain, aside from the sting of his bite and someday, the birth of his children.

That thought spurred him on and he started to pound into her faster, eager to fill her with his seed.

"Callie, we didn't, are you on anything?"

"Yes, don't stop," she assured him.

He was glad she was protected because more than anything he wanted to know his seed was inside of her, scenting her so any shifter they passed would know; she was his.

"Mick," she gasped, her hands on his neck, she was pulling him closer and meeting his thrusts, she was close, he could feel it in the way her body clenched his cock.

"You're ready to be mine, in all ways?" he whispered in her ear.

"Yes, Mick I want to be your everything."

He didn't wait for anything else. He sat up, pulling her with him, her legs wrapped around his waist, his cock buried inside her clenching cunt and he dipped his head to her neck. His teeth were long, ready to pierce skin. He slipped a hand between their bodies and pinched her clit, pushing her over the edge and as she gasped her pleasure he struck. He bit into her skin and when he tasted her blood his wolf howled, and the magic of the mating bond flowed between them. Suddenly his body was on fire with awareness, beyond what had struck the first time he'd scented her. This awareness was so complete he could feel her heartbeat as if it were in his own chest, her breath as if it were in his own lungs and her pleasure, ratcheting his own to heights never reached.

He tore his mouth from her neck and howled at the ceiling as he thrust one last time and filled her with his seed.

"My mate," he growled, gathering her close and laying down with her as they both breathed heavy, sweat soaked bodies trembling around each other. He licked her wounds clean and watched them disappear, visible only to a shifter, they marked her as his.

CHAPTER 25

CALLIE

Callie woke up in Mick's arms. Her neck felt bruised, her body felt well fucked, and her heart felt full. She opened her eyes and found Mick staring at her, a thoughtful look on his face.

"How do you feel?" he asked, brushing a hair from her face and tucking it behind her ear.

"I feel ..." she paused and realized not only did she feel amazing, but she felt him, a nervous energy that wasn't hers and a love so deep it scared and comforted her. "I feel you inside me," she gasped.

His smile was wide and bright. "That's the mating bond."

"Oh, Mick, I can't believe you're real." And she couldn't believe the love she was feeling was real, it was coming from him, it was his love for her, and she could feel it so clearly. "Will it always be like this?" It was almost overwhelming. She couldn't imagine going to work and feeling this, she'd never be able to concentrate.

"I think you get used to it. You'll be able to sort of compartmentalize it and of course, when we aren't laying naked next to each other it might not be so intense," he said with a wolfish grin.

She wanted to indulge in the promise of that grin, but the sun was up and she knew that Taylor would be soon too, if he wasn't already.

"What now?" she asked. They hadn't really discussed the details of this relationship beyond this commitment.

"You and Taylor will join the pack," he said as if it were obvious, but his expression and the feelings she was able to access of his, told her that there was anxiety and worry beneath it. He was afraid of her rejecting the rest of him, his pack and lifestyle.

She smiled and kissed him. "Of course we will, I just didn't want to assume."

His grin was wide and sweet. "Assume that everything in my life is now yours, including a wolf shifter pack. There's a bit of responsibility that will come with being the alpha's mate."

"I'm sure I can handle that."

He kissed her and moaned against her lips. "Callie, I love you and I believe you can handle anything," he said the words she had already felt flowing through him.

"I love you too, Mick."

"Does this mean we are going back?" Taylor yelled through the closed door.

"Sure does!" Mick answered.

"Yes!" Taylor yelled and ran down the hall.

"Did you know he was there?" she asked.

"Yes, which is the only reason my cock isn't buried inside you right now."

Callie rolled her eyes but she was laughing. "I guess that means it's time to get up. I hope you can handle being a full-time dad. It means we can't stay in bed having wild sex all day every day."

"While I disagree with your assessment—because we can definitely send Taylor to spend some nights and days with his Auntie Tara and Uncle Kody—I can handle anything if it means I get to have you in my arms every night."

"Forever," she agreed, and she meant it and it didn't feel like too much, it didn't feel like she was giving up any part of herself at all, it felt like she was sharing herself with him, trusting him with her most delicate self, and gaining the same from him.

This is what a partnership was meant to be, she felt it down to her soul.

MEET THE AUTHOR

Courtney Davis is an author, mother, wife and teacher living in North Idaho. She loves to spend her time creating stories to take readers on adventures full of excitement, and love.